Other books by Cheryl Russell

Lily of the Valley

The Necklace

Evening Treats A collection of short stories

Gallows Lane

The One Who Got Away

A Bruised Reed

Missing

Murderous Feet

A Place of Safety

Chapter One

"Mummy, mummy I've lost teddy. We have to go back."

"Shush darling, we have to be very quiet. We can't go back, it's not safe, we must carry on. You have to be brave and a big girl like daddy said."

Eve picked up her daughter and almost ran forward. She needed to put as much distance between them and their pursuers as she could. She really wanted to catch a train but it was too risky. They would check that and drag them off. She couldn't risk getting caught. They had to reach the convent then they would be safe, until they could be smuggled out of France.

Finally the convent was in sight, she ran the last little way and rang the bell. She just about hung on until the gate was opened then she collapsed onto the ground. Safe at last!

....

Opening her eyes Eve looked around disorientated. Where was she? She saw someone sitting by her bed dressed like a nun.

"Hello," said Eve tentatively.

"You're back with us then," said the nun.

"Where am I?"

"You are in the convent of St Mary's on the outskirts of Nice."

Memories started flooding back to Eve and she gasped. "Francesca," she cried.

"It's all right. She's safe and being looked after. It's you we've been so worried about. You have been unconscious for five days now. The doctor said it was all the stress and trauma."

"The doctor? No, we have to leave now. It's not safe for us to stay here and we're putting you in danger."

"Don't worry. The doctor is always ready to help with our guests if needed. He's safe."

Eve relaxed back onto the pillow and sighed. She couldn't believe it had been five days ago that William had come home from work and said they had to leave immediately. They had known it was coming and had stuff packed in bags. They were taking as little as possible because it would be strange and could be questioned if they carried suitcases. It had to look as normal as possible.

A colleague of Williams's had warned him that his name was on the list for that day. He worked in the police and had managed to keep his job somehow even when all Jews were to be sacked with immediate effect. Being in the police it was easy to see who were on the list. Forewarned he rushed straight home to his family. It was now that he wished he'd never left England to live in France with his French wife. If only he had insisted they move to England. How easy it was to see in hindsight though. Back in 1930 it had never been an issue. No one could have foreseen the tension and evil that would appear in Germany and that a crazed dictator would want to conquer the world as Hitler seemed bent on doing.

William hadn't been so lucky. He had stayed behind just by a few minutes to lock the door and then turned to follow his family, only to find himself face to face with Germans. It was too late. Eve, hearing the noise had turned round in time to see William being pushed on to the truck that would carry him away to God knows where.

Eve hurried away not wanting Francesca to see what was happening to her daddy. They had to put enough distance between them or they would be caught as well. It seemed they had got away in the nick of time.

"Francesca! I need to see her," said Eve.

"You need to rest and get your strength back first. She's fine. Happily playing with the other children."

"Other children?"

"Don't worry," said Sister Monique. "We have four families as guests at the moment. She's playing with them inside. We don't allow our guests outside in case a German patrol happens to go by. Fortunately at the moment we are being left alone so we can continue in our work of saving God's chosen people. You just relax and try and have some of this soup. It's a beef broth. Here's some water for you to drink as well. Just take small sips that's right."

Eve was too weak to protest and lay back on the pillows letting Sister Monique spoon the thick broth into her mouth. She chewed and swallowed automatically not tasting the nourishing food. Her thoughts were miles away with her husband wondering if he was still alive and where he was. What was he going through? Was he thinking of her and worried about their daughter? They heard so many bad things these days. People disappearing and never being heard from again. It had happened with their neighbours just last week.

"Can you hear me?" asked the pleasant faced nun.

Eve shook her head. "Sorry I was miles away. Thinking about my husband. Is there anyway of finding out what happened to him after the Germans took him?"

The nun looked grave but her kindly eyes were full of compassion. "I'll try and find out for you but I can't promise anything. It's not safe to ask too many questions and I have to put my nuns and other guests first."

"I understand. I'm sorry I asked."

"You don't need to apologise. It's only natural you want answers. Tell me about your husband."

"He was a loving family orientated man. In the police. I'm blaming myself as he wouldn't be in this position if it wasn't for me. You see he's English. He agreed to move here when we married because I didn't want to live in England."

The sister looked grave as she listened. She had noticed that Eve had changed tense in her speech. How difficult it must be, the not knowing must be the worst.

Sister Monique stood up and looked down on the white faced woman in the bed. "You rest now while I put out some feelers. I'll look in on you later."

She closed the door quietly and went to the kitchen with the empty bowl on her way to the Mother Superior.

Mother Marie looked up with a smile when she saw Monique in the doorway. "How's the patient today?"

"She's awake and just had all the broth. She's asking about her husband though who was taken."

Marie shook her head sadly. "We are hearing too many stories like this every day. We can't help everyone you know that. It was just unfortunate they arrived as the family left."

"How do you know?" asked Monique stunned.

"I like to keep my finger on the pulse. Not much happens without my knowledge you should know that by now."

"I know, but this is far more."

"I don't know what you should tell her. Her husband was last seen being forcibly pushed onto a cattle truck and being taken off. Probably to one of those camps we hear too much about. There is nothing we can do except pray for those poor souls." Marie sighed as if she had the weight of the world on her shoulders, which she did. There was too much evil in the world at that present moment and no sign of it coming to an end.

Monique's eyes filled with tears. She was a sensitive person who felt everyone's pain. "I think she deserves to know the truth."

"If you think she can handle it then tell her."

"The truth is best, at least she has answers and doesn't hope for what may never happen. People go in those cattle trucks are never heard from again and we have to face facts here."

"I agree. By all means tell her and I will be praying."

"I'm not sure I believe in prayer anymore. I can't believe in a loving God who allows this to happen to His chosen people."

"I know what you mean but every time I ask the same questions I am reminded that we have free will and that means evil in this world. It is not of God, He cries with us as He sees the pain."

"I wish I could believe it but I can't."

"I will pray for you. My door is always open if you want to talk through your doubts."

"Thank you." Monique curtsied and left the room closing the door quietly.

She sighed as she looked up the stairs thinking of that poor woman. Life was so hard for so many people these days and they just couldn't help everyone.

"How is that woman?" asked a voice behind her.

She turned and looked at Sister Eunice saying, "Not good. All we can do is pray for her."

Eunice shook her head, "What is this world coming to?"

"I don't know really," said Monique. "Anyway I can't stand here gossiping. I have things to do."

She moved away abruptly. She had no time for the other nun, there was something shifty about her. You could see it in the eyes. She shivered slightly feeling as if someone had just walked over her grave. She climbed the stairs to see if Eve was awake. She was thinking of the conversation she was to have which made her reluctant to continue. Eve already looked worried to death without the news she had to impart.

Just reaching Eve's room she heard a whistle blow. Her heart began hammering in her chest as she glanced out of the window and saw the Germans at the gate. She knew she had only a few minutes before they would be in and searching the place. Thinking quickly she rushed into Eve's room.

"Hurry up the Germans are here. Quick get out of bed and kneel as if in prayer. I'll kneel with you and will start saying the Hail Mary when they come in here."

Picking up on the urgency in Monique's voice she did as urged. She was shaky from fear as much as from lack of adequate nourishment the last few days. She needed time to get her strength back.

It wasn't long before they heard the thunderous sound of footsteps on the stairs. The door burst open banging sharply against the wall. Eve jumped but Monique laid a calming hand on her.

"Stand," shouted a commanding voice.

Monique started out loud to repeat "Hail Mary."

"Shut that noise. You speak when I say and not before. We don't want to hear any of your Catholic rubbish. You worship Adolf Hitler our dear Fuhrer and no one else. Do you hear me?"

Monique nodded, but continued moving her lips silently.

"We have reports of a Jewish lady coming here with a child. Where is she hiding? I know she is here somewhere."

"I don't know what you mean," said Monique.

She could feel Eve shaking next to her and knew she had to be strong for the both of them.

"What about you?" he said pointing to Eve.

Eve opened her mouth but no sound came out.

"Come on then. Answer. Are you dumb?"

Monique jumped in for her, saying, "She isn't well. She lost her voice yesterday. We are awaiting the doctor to check her over."

"Hmm!" sighed the German disbelievingly, before leaving the room.

Monique breathed a sigh of relief, but inwardly she knew the danger was not over. He could return anytime.

As Monique thought about it she felt angry and worried. She needed to speak to the Mother Superior as soon as possible about her fears. If she were right they were all in deep trouble.

The danger passed at least for then. They were all aware the Germans could return and most probably would now they were on their radar.

Chapter Two

"Please I must speak with you Mother," said Monique bursting in the room without knocking or bobbing the regulation curtsy.

Marie looked fiercely at her but said nothing. Monique was obviously in quite a state so she was let off just the once.

"It's urgent or I wouldn't have bothered you at this time," said Monique.

"Speak," said Marie. This was so unlike Monique that Marie ignored the lack of manners and common curtesy.

"I think we have a traitor in our midst. The Germans knew about Eve and Francesca."

"A traitor? That's a bit strong isn't it?"

"How else could they have known?"

"They could have seen them."

"Then why not come earlier. Remember as well, that they arrived in pitch darkness."

"True," said Monique feeling slightly foolish.

"Who is this traitor? Presumably you have some proof."

"Eunice," said Monique. "She stopped me and started questioning me about Eve. Only a short while later the Germans are at our gate."

"I see your point but you can't make accusations like that without some proof."

Monique didn't reply, but she continued looking at Marie who seemed lost in thought.

There was silence for a few minutes before Marie spoke, "I was told we had a disabled Jewish child here."

Monique gasped, "You see. How would they have known that."

"You're making sense. I just can't believe any of my nuns would behave like this."

"Who knows how anyone would react until they face such circumstances."

"You're right." Marie sighed. "Do you have any suspicions as to who it is?"

Monique nodded, but was reluctant to voice it. She felt guilty making such a serious allegation.

Sensing the fight going on in Monique's mind, Marie kept silent, waiting until Monique felt able to say. Marie was a wise leader of the community of nuns. She knew when to keep quiet and when to probe deeper and this was the time to say nothing.

At last Monique spoke, it was just a whisper and Marie had to lean forward to catch the words. "I still think it's Eunice. She seemed a bit too interested in Eve earlier."

"Eunice! Surely not."

"Unfortunately I think so."

"Now if you had said Belle I would have believed it, but Eunice. I know she can be a bit abrupt and nosy but a traitor I don't see it."

"I don't think it can be a coincidence when shortly after that conversation with Eunice the Germans arrive on our doorstep. They've never bothered us before."

"Yes, but it was only a matter of time before they did. We couldn't expect to avoid them permanently. We just have to be extra vigilant."

"So you don't think it's a traitor in our midst?"

"I don't think we have enough evidence as yet. Leave it with me, I have some thinking to do."

Monique nodded and seeing the interview was at an end left the room with the regulation curtsey. She wasn't fooled. She had a feeling of satisfaction and a lightening in her spirit. She knew Marie would work something out and it would all work for the best.

Indeed Marie was using her brain to do some serious thinking. She needed to find out if it really was Eunice. Maybe feeding her some wrong information would be a test. Something that would make Eunice run to the Germans if in fact it was her. She would have to be careful how she did it. It had to look as if she bumped into her accidentally. Eunice would surely be suspicious if she were to send for her and then tell her. She had to think of something serious enough to warrant telling the occupying forces. She gave the matter more thought and then gave a grim smile to herself. She had an idea and, if indeed Eunice was a traitor she would soon know. Before saying anything to Eunice she needed to speak to Monique again.

Something had to be sorted out to keep Eve safe first. She wasn't prepared to compromise the safety of anyone under her care.

Monique bobbed as usual as she entered.

"I've found a way to test Eunice but I need to ensure Eve stays safe. I don't want to risk them seeing Eve as she was earlier. My suggestion is to dress her up as a nun and quickly give her a run down on the behaviour of a nun so she doesn't stand out at all. It would be wrong to hide her away now the Germans have seen her and believe her to be one of us. That would just give rise to more suspicion. The Germans aren't stupid by any means."

"That's fine I can do that of course," said Monique. "My concern would be that Eunice would be suspicious as she would wonder where the extra nun had come from and that really could cause problems for us."

Marie looked downcast, she hadn't thought of that. "Try and keep Eve away from Eunice for now."

Monique nodded. How she hated this subterfuge but something had to be done. If Eunice were indeed a traitor then she was dangerous. She didn't envy Marie that job. What could be done if they could get the proof?

Marie was wrestling with that very same thought. What to do with a traitor which wouldn't make the Germans even more suspicious?

It was dinner time before Marie had a genuine chance to speak to Eunice. "You're not going to believe this. I've just heard via our network that we are to have an influx of Jewish children coming tonight, under cover of darkness. I'll be relying on you to look after them and get them settled."

"Where are their parents?"

"I don't know. I can't ask as I wouldn't be told anyway. It's a need to know basis. It's safer that way."

Eunice finished her dinner quickly then asked to be excused on the pretext of making preparations for the children. Monique and Marie looked at each other meaningfully. They were sure where Eunice was really going.

It was nine in the evening when the first signs of activity occurred. Trucks were pulling up outside the convent and then the sounds of jack boots on the cobbles could be heard. The nuns looked at each other as they continued with their recreation. More than one of them looked scared. They all knew it was the Germans. Eve, alone in her room, felt scared. She was dressed as a nun and had been told to join them at the first signs of trouble. She went slowly downstairs where she met Monique who was waiting for her.

"It's going to be ok," whispered Monique.

"I can't help it. Even though you warned me this would happen I still can't help but be scared. I'm Jewish, an enemy of the Third Reich. If anything happens to me you will look after Francesca and keep her safe won't you."

"Of course I will," said Monique putting a reassuring arm on Eve's. "You've got nothing to worry about. This is a place of safety, or as close as it can be in these dangerous times."

Eve gave a wobbly smile. Together with Monique she left the small, bare room. The room was definitely minimalist, showing the simple life of the nuns and their devotion to God.

Eve shyly followed Monique into the room and sat down stiffly next to her. The other nuns looked curiously at her but said nothing. In these days all sorts of strange things were happening. Nothing phased them anymore.

Loud voices could be heard as the door crashed against the wall as it was opened.

"Where are the Jews?" shouted a German who appeared to be in charge.

"We don't know what you're talking about," said Monique, the only one with the courage to face the German officer.

"What's all this about," asked Marie entering the room calmly. "You are disturbing the nuns recreation and meditation time."

"We are here for the Jews."

"What Jews? We are all Catholic nuns here."

"The Jewish children you're expecting tonight." Turning to the other officers he commanded, "Search the place from top to bottom. They are here I know they are. I can smell a rotten Jew a mile off. Leave no stone unturned. We are not leaving here without the Jews."

"There are no Jews," said Marie again.

"QUIET!" shouted the German.

Monique and Marie exchanged knowing looks but said nothing. All they could do was wait until they'd gone then they would have to discuss the way forward. It seemed obvious now that Eunice really was the traitor in their midst. Marie felt a heavy heart. What was she to do with her? It would have to be something subtle so as not to make the Germans suspicious. She was also wary about accepting more Jews as it was starting to become dangerous for all concerned. Now the Germans had them on their radar there was no telling what would happen next. There would be many more visits of that she was certain.

The men came back and shook their heads at the commanding officer.

"Nothing. They are here somewhere I just know it. They must be. Are you sure you searched thoroughly. They must be hidden away somewhere."

The men shook their heads. The place was clean. Nothing suspicious anywhere.

"I don't trust you. I think I should take someone in for questioning."

"If you want to take anyone take me," said Marie.

The officer shook his head. "I choose whom I take no one else."

He looked around the room, eyeing them fiercely. Many of the nuns drew back intimidated and not wanting to catch his eye. Who knew what horrors they would be subjected to if they were taken. They wouldn't even know if they would be sent back to the convent or if they would just disappear like so many people were these days. Never to be heard from again.

His eyes lit on Eve. "That one," he said pointing.

Eve shrank next to Monique. Monique stood up, "I'll go with you," she said.

He shook his head and insisted on Eve. "Well come on, stand up. You're coming with us," he commanded.

Eve stood not believing this was happening. This was supposed to have been a place of safety and now look. She was struck by the irony of the situation. Here she was a Jew in hiding with a group of nuns and she was still taken by the German monsters who believed they were taking a Catholic nun.

Marie kept her face impassive. This was where all the work they had done to provide a safe haven for the Jews could be undone. Out of all the nuns they could have chosen, they chose the Jew among them.

Suddenly there was a shuffling at the back as Belle forced her way forward. "Take me I'm really a Jew. It's me you want. The nuns knew nothing about my background when I arrived. They are not to be blamed."

"How long have you been here?"

"Since 1938," said Belle. "I came when it became obvious the way things were going. You had just occupied Austria. I thought if I became a nun I would be safe."

"In that case I'll take you as well. I don't trust you so I'm still taking this one too."

He grabbed the two women and roughly thrust them forward in front of him. The two women went without a backward glance. Eve, head down was terrified but Belle held her head up high.

Belle was confident they wouldn't be able to prove either way who she really was because her family had died just after she entered the convent. None of her old friends would recognise her now, and anyway the convent was the other side of France to where she had come from, which was just the way she liked it.

Chapter Three

"Eunice can I have a word please?"

Eunice turned startled at Marie's tone of voice. It sounded so serious. Quickly she went through the past few hours to see what sin she had committed. She couldn't think of anything that would warrant such a serious call from Marie. She followed reluctantly to Marie's room.

"Sit down," said Marie in the same serious tone.

"Have I done something wrong?" asked Eunice in a small voice.

"I don't know. Have you?"

"I don't think so."

"Have you made any phone calls today?"

Eunice so surprised at this question shook her head without speaking.

"Speak when I ask you a question," said Marie sternly.

"N…no," said Eunice, becoming frightened, not having a clue where this was going.

"Someone has."

"Sorry, it wasn't me."

"Is that the truth? Or are you realising the seriousness of your actions and are too scared to tell me?"

"It's the truth. I wouldn't lie. I've never told a lie even when it's meant I'm in trouble."

Marie nodded, realising that to be true. Eunice was the one person whom she could trust to be completely honest about anything. Maybe that was why she had been so reluctant to believe Eunice capable of collaborating with the Germans. She was now starting to realise she had made a terrible mistake. She shouldn't have been swayed by Monique but by her own judgement. Yet Monique had to be right, there was someone informing the Germans of what was happening at the convent. All she was now aware of was that it wasn't Eunice. She needed to find out who it was before they were put in more danger.

"You may go but don't speak of this conversation to anyone. It's important," warned Marie.

Greatly daring, Eunice said, "Can't you tell me what's going on. I think you owe me that much after appearing to accuse me of something."

"I don't owe you any explanation. In this case it's best as few people as possible know what's happening so it doesn't leak to the perpetrator."

"This sounds mysterious but I'll bow to your judgement of course."

"Thank you. Could you send Monique to me please?"

Eunice nodded, opened the door and left the room. She breathed a sigh of relief. She had thought she had been in real trouble then.

Looking for Monique she wondered what was going on that was so top secret. She supposed it could have something to do with the Jews as Marie kept things connected with them close to her chest. Yes, they all knew they were there but details they didn't know. How they arrived. Where they went when they left and who helped were secrets that no one else knew. They all agreed it was the safest way to proceed.

"Ah there you are," said Eunice having found Monique at last. "Mother wants to see you."

"Ok I'll go straight there."

"I better warn you she's in a strange mood."

"Thanks. I don't think I've done anything wrong though."

"Neither have I, but that hasn't stopped her thinking I may have done."

Monique made a noncommittal sound. She was guessing what it was about.

She hurriedly made her way to Marie, hoping to hear some positive news.

Knocking on the door she was called to enter. She went in and took a seat that Marie indicated without speaking. Marie still had that serious look on her face that she'd had when she had the interview with Eunice.

"I take it you've spoken to Eunice," said Monique without giving Marie a chance to speak.

"I asked if she had made any phone calls today. I didn't want to give away what I was really asking about, especially if she were the one. She says she hasn't made any today. She seemed quite surprised at the way the interview went."

"You don't believe her do you?" asked Monique.

"Yes I think I do," said Marie quietly. "As she pointed out she has never lied. I believe you about the traitor in our midst, but I'm convinced it's not Eunice.

"But who then?"

Marie shrugged, at a complete loss. "I don't know. You don't think it's Eve do you?"

"Eve!" exclaimed Monique.

"Yes, she's the latest person to come and we've only had problems since she arrived."

"But she's a Jew. That makes her an enemy of the Reich. Besides she's been arrested."

"She says she's a Jew but we only have her word for it. For all we know she was planted here and she's really a Nazi spy."

Monique gasped. "She's been arrested though."

"That doesn't mean anything. We don't know how they treated her once she was out of here do we."

Monique shook her head. "I don't agree. She's who she says she is, I'm sure of it. She's too traumatised by what she's been through lately."

"That could all be an act."

"Do you really believe it's Eve."

Marie shook her head and sighed, "I don't know what to believe anymore. All I really know it's someone here and I don't want to think it could be one of my nuns."

Monique understood where Marie was coming from. It would be very hard if it turned out to be one of the community that they had lived with for years. Marie had been there for twenty years and knew everyone of her nuns inside out, or so she thought. What had made one of them turn collaborator all of a sudden? Monique had been there almost as long and she was close in age to Marie which made them friends, or as much as friends as they were allowed. Particular friendships were not encouraged in the religious life. Marie did have a habit of confiding in Monique though and she trusted Monique implicitly. So much so that it didn't occur to her that Monique could be the informer. In her view it was anyone but.

"We can't take anymore Jews until this gets sorted out. It would be too risky. I've also been in touch with my contacts to let them know what the situation is. At the beginning we agreed on a code so I've been able to use that without alerting anyone who may be listening whether it be a collaborator or a German. They are going to try and get the Jews out of here if it's deemed safe to do so."

Monique nodded. "What about Eve, she's still with the Germans along with Belle."

"We can't do anything about Eve now except pray for her." Marie sighed before adding, "This was meant to be a place of safety but look what it's turned out to be, far from it."

"Once we deal with the traitor it will be once again," said Monique trying to reassure Marie.

"Will it? I'll find it very hard to trust anyone. This has really shaken me up. I was so sure all my nuns were trustworthy."

"If that's all you want to discuss I feel I should go to the chapel and pray," said Monique standing up.

Marie nodded. "We'll need all the prayers we can if we are to get through this alive."

Monique left the room and went in the direction of the chapel.

Chapter Four

"Ok tell me your real name?" barked the German. He was the same commanding officer who had led the search of the convent. He decided he wanted to interview the women himself. He didn't believe for one minute that Belle was Jewish. The other one though he couldn't be sure. There was something about her that put his back up. He had decided to interview her first.

"Evangelique," whispered Eve.

"Speak up," he growled.

Eve repeated her name this time louder.

"Tell me what is going on at the convent. I know something is."

"How can you be sure?" asked Eve bravely.

"I have my sources. I have a reach anywhere I choose. Plenty of people are willing to cooperate, believing it will give them an easier life under the Third Reich."

Eve's mind began spinning. It sounded as if there was a traitor at the convent who was giving things away. If only she could get back there and warn them. It wasn't safe for the nuns or the Jews hiding there. It seemed best to her that she be released. How could she make that happen though. She was at this awful man's mercy. It was what he wanted.

"Answer my question when I speak to you," he ordered.

"Sorry can you repeat the question please?" she asked politely.

He sighed and looked at her. "You should have been paying attention and not wasting my time. I'm a busy man you know."

"I'm sorry I'm the wrong person to be asking as I'm actually new to the convent. I know very little about what goes on there. I came from another convent in Paris. I only arrived last week."

Eve was thinking on the top of her head. She was struggling to come up with answers that she honestly couldn't expect to know having just arrived herself as a Jewish refugee wanting to get to England and safety.

"Hmm," he said. He was becoming more suspicious by the minute of this so called nun. Definitely a Jew, he just had to prove it. It was typical of a Jew to be so stupid to say she was new to the convent. They clearly had no brains. How they managed to feed off the true Aryans he had no idea. She wasn't a German Jew though. Her accent definitely said she was French. He felt he could now prove they were hiding Jews at the convent. Where he couldn't possibly say as they never found any in their searches, except for this one.

He stood up and moving to the door requested she be taken back to the cells. Grabbed by her arm she was dragged along the corridor and down some stairs she was roughly pushed into the cell. It was cold and damp down there in what appeared to be a basement. Eve involuntarily shivered, not just because of the cold but through fear as well. She suspected the General who had interviewed her knew she was Jewish although he hadn't said so outright. What would happen to her? Moreover, what would happen to Francesca without her parents. She was too young to be an orphan. Would the nuns continue to look after her? She should have sorted this out with the Mother Superior beforehand so she could have some hope of reassurance as to Francesca's future. If there were to be one for a Jew. The Germans didn't care if it was a child or not all that mattered was getting rid of all Jews full stop.

She tried to lay on the cold, hard uneven slabs on the ground to close her eyes. She was so tired having not yet recovered from her collapse. She found she couldn't sleep. There was too much noise of people shouting and some screams of agony. This frightened Eve further. Did they torture people here as well? Would that happen to her?

Nausea rose within forcing her to retch but nothing came up. The convent was supposed to be a safe haven until they could be got to England. She really needed to get back to warn them that they had a traitor in their midst. How to do that was a problem. It relied on the Germans deciding to let her go but she couldn't see that happening any time soon. They were too suspicious and they wanted information.

She sat huddled in the corner wondering if she could give them some false details. That still wouldn't work because it would be admitting that they were hiding Jews. She was not prepared to give anything away that made them work that out.

The door opened, interrupting Eve's thoughts. Belle was thrust inside with her. Belle crawled over to Eve.

"Are you all right?" asked Eve with some concern.

Belle nodded grimly but didn't speak.

"We need to get out of here," said Eve. "I think there's a traitor at the convent who is tipping the Germans off as to their activities."

"Oh and how do you intend doing that? We're stuck here at the mercy of those evil men in case you hadn't noticed," said Belle with a touch of sarcasm in her voice.

"I don't know," said Eve starting to give into despair.

"Hey, I'm sorry, I didn't mean to upset you. I'm just so frustrated and frightened myself and lashed out. I know it must be worse for you."

Eve nodded.

"Of course if you're the informer you have nothing to be scared of," said Eve after the silence had been going on for more than a few minutes.

"It's not me, I promise you that."

"You would say that though wouldn't you. You wouldn't want me telling them at the convent. The repercussions would be serious."

"I'm telling you the truth. It isn't me."

"Maybe, maybe not. I don't know what I believe. My head's all over the place."

"Same here," said Belle quietly. She hoped to get across to Eve that she was safe with her. Her secret wouldn't get out to the enemy.

"Look I'm sorry," said Eve. "I didn't mean to accuse you. I'm sure you're innocent or you wouldn't be here. The Germans surely couldn't arrest their informant or they would get no more information from them."

"It's ok. We're both under pressure and frightened."

Eve felt relieved. It wasn't good for either of them to have an atmosphere between them in their situation. They needed to work together if they were to be freed.

It was at that moment the door crashed open. "Come with me," the German barked at Eve.

Eve stood up slowly, cold and exhausted. She just wanted to go back to the relative comfort of the convent. Even in the convent's austere lifestyle it was better than the cell they found themselves in.

"Hurry up."

Eve went as fast as she could. She found herself going along a different corridor leading to another locked door. It was opened and she was pushed through it and the door locked behind her. She looked around her and breathed a sigh of relief. She was outside. Although being unfamiliar to the area had no idea how to get back to the convent.

There were people around but they gave Eve a wide berth. This shouldn't have been a surprise when she looked at herself. She was wearing the nuns outfit but it was creased and dirty after sitting in that awful cell. She was completely dishevelled.

"Can I help you sister," asked a voice from beside her.

Eve turned and saw a child beside her. She nodded. "Can you tell me the way back to the convent please. I'm completely lost."

"I'll take you if you like. But we have to hurry I'm only supposed to be a few minutes."

The girl reached her hand to take hold of Eve's. She was only to happy to feel the warmth of a friendly person. She knew how quickly that could disappear for good. Before they moved away the girl looked all around her, careful in case they were being followed. No one seemed to be paying them any attention but that didn't mean anything.

"What's your name?" asked Eve wanting to be friendly.

"Mathilde."

"That's a nice name."

"I was named after my grandmere. Come on it's down this way," said Mathilde, tugging at Eve's hand and taking her down an alley.

Eve followed. She found she needed all her breath to keep up with Mathilde who was almost running. They went down what seemed like a maze of tiny, narrow streets.

"This is the quickest route and the best if you want to avoid the Germans," said Mathilde, who seemed a friendly child who just wanted to help.

It wasn't long before Mathilde true to her word, stopped outside the convent. Turning away she quickly ran off without saying goodbye. Eve turned round to thank her but the child was nowhere to be found.

She rung the bell and didn't have long to wait before Eunice opened the door. "Oh you poor girl!" she exclaimed as she let Eve in. "You look frozen and distraught. What must you have been through. Come in."

Eve stepped inside and sank into the nearest chair with a sigh of relief.

"I'll go and get Mother Superior," she said.

"No please don't leave me. I can't."

"She needs to know you are back and you look like you need a good hot meal inside you."

Eve said nothing. She felt if she were to put anything inside at that moment she would bring it straight back up again.

It was at that time that Monique came hurrying up to them. "You're back. Oh thank God for His mercy," she said and crossed herself. "We've been praying for you. You're on your own. Where's Belle?"

Eve shrugged. "I don't know what happened. We were together in the cell but I was dragged out and dumped outside that awful place. I don't know what happened to her."

Monique crossed herself again and said, "We must continue to pray for her."

"Come on you're coming with me first to Mother then to your room and bed. You looked washed out," she said with some concern, looking at the pale face of Eve.

"I am rather."

Monique and Eunice helped Eve to her feet and tried to help her get to Marie's room. It soon became obvious that it wasn't going to happen. Eve was too shaken up and worn out.

"You stay with her," said Eunice, "I'll go and get Mother."

Marie and Eunice rushed to Eve's side. Marie knelt down by Eve and looked her up and down. She was concerned by the greyish pallor. "Oh you poor dear, what must you have been through."

She held up her hand as Eve tried to speak. "No don't speak yet. There's time for that later. You need some food inside you and a good sleep."

"No, no I must tell you something first. It's important," Eve managed to gasp out.

"Right you two go and set a place for Eve at the table and get some soup warmed up. That will get some nourishment into her."

When the two nuns had gone to obey Marie's orders she turned back to Eve and said, "What's troubling you my dear that can't wait."

"I think you have a traitor here."

Marie nodded, not looking at all surprised.

"You know?"

"Yes. Monique worked it out before you got dragged off with Belle."

"Do you know who it is?"

Marie shook her head. "We thought we did but we were wrong. Have you any idea?"

Eve shook her head. "It was just a thought I had and I knew I somehow had to get a message to you for you to deal with before anyone else is put at risk."

"Thank you, I really appreciate the thought."

"I had to say something. You are good people and I don't want to see you in trouble or what you do to help my people having to stop. There aren't many people like you around. Most people are too scared of falling foul of the Gestapo. While they occupy this beautiful country lives are at risk."

Marie nodded. "Now come with me and try and eat something. I know you don't feel hungry but you will feel better for it. We can talk again later."

Eve let Marie help her up and help her to the dining hall. She collapsed on to the chair and picked up the spoon began to eat. It was only when she started that she realised how hungry she really was. The three nuns noticed and were satisfied that given time she would be fine. Good food and rest were what she needed after all she had been through.

"When do you think Belle will be back?" asked Monique in a whisper, not wanting Eve to overhear.

Marie shook her head, "Your guess is as good as mine on that one. Let's hope it won't be long. What concerns me is that they let Eve go and not Belle."

"You don't still believe Eve is our traitor do you?" asked Monique.

"No," said Marie. "I think she's genuine, but we do need to find out who it is and quickly before anything else happens."

Eunice said, "Could it be Belle? She's been gone a long time and she isn't back yet."

"I don't think the Germans would keep her that long if she were, as they would want her back here ready to pass any information on. I still can't believe there is an informant in our midst. It's making me question everything I knew about everyone here."

"I know," said Monique. "I look at everyone and wonder if it's them."

"That was delicious," said Eve, breaking into their conversation.

She had eaten the whole bowl and drunk the milky coffee she had been given. She gave a yawn.

"Come on, you're worn out. Let's help you to your room then you can have a good sleep."

Eve nodded, too tired to do anything else. She felt completely washed out. She hated to think how Belle must be feeling or what she was going through having been kept there as a prisoner. Had the Gestapo spoken to her. If so what had they done to her. They were known to be brutal in their tactics to extract information from people.

The three nuns helped Eve up the stairs and into bed. It wasn't a comfortable bed in keeping with the austere conditions the nuns lived in. The mattress was rock hard but Eve didn't care. All she wanted was to sleep and try and forget what she had been through. She knew she was lucky, they hadn't used any underhanded tactics to get her to confess to anything. She still couldn't work out why she had been let go and not Belle.

Back downstairs the three nuns were together in Marie's room having a conflab about the traitor in their midst.

"We need to be extra vigilant," said Marie. "We need to work out who it is before they can inform on us again. I'm still inclined to believe that it isn't a nun. It could be one of the Jews who is only pretending to be a Jew."

"I don't think we can rule anyone out at this point," said Monique.

"It must be someone. We can't go around making accusations against anyone when we don't really have anything to go on. To speak to the wrong person could alert the real informant that we are on to them, unless of course it is Belle."

"Could it be one of the staff that comes in just for the day to do the cleaning or cooking."

"I hadn't thought of that. It could very well be. I would prefer it if it were them because at least then they would know that their days were numbered and it would be easy to get rid of them."

"Which would be difficult if it were one of us."

"Exactly," said Marie.

"Come on let's all go to bed. There is nothing more we can achieve tonight," said Monique, with a yawn.

"I agree," said Marie. "We will be able to think more clearly in the morning when we're fresh. We know it has to be someone. Until whomever it is has been dealt with I don't think we can risk taking anymore Jews in. We don't want them to be put at risk. It wouldn't be fair when they think they are coming to a place of safety, only to find they are in more danger by being here."

Monique shook her head. "I really don't know what's for the best, but I'll go along with what you say if that is your decision. It seems so sad that we can't go on rescuing God's chosen people. I really felt we were doing something important in His service."

"I understand," said Marie. "I won't do anything lightly, but I can't have peoples lives put at risk. It would be wrong."

"What about those we have with us at the moment? Also if we stop taking Jews won't the traitor get suspicious then it might lead to more trouble. We are lucky the Germans allow us to continue in our worship of God. We can't expect that to continue indefinitely. Not now that we have come to their notice," said Eunice.

"I need to think and pray before doing anything drastic," said Marie. "Now let's get to bed. We need to sleep."

Chapter Five

Eve lay there half awake and half dozing. She hadn't slept well and when she had been asleep she was disturbed by nightmares about her time with the Germans. Was it really a good idea to stay in the convent? Would they all be taken and put in one of the camps they all knew about but never mentioned in conversations. She and Francesca, now rested could continue there journey to the border. Once over the border it should make it much easier to make their way to England. They would be safe there she knew. It was getting there that was the problem.

The bell sounded which was the sign that prayers were due. She decided to go to the small service anyway. Even though she didn't, as a Jew, believe in Jesus Christ as saviour she needed peace which she had discovered in this place, the chapel especially. She couldn't get used to being woken up so early though. It left her like a zombie during the day.

"Well ladies, there are no signs of Belle being returned yet. In fact we've heard nothing more which could be a good or bad sign. I am thinking ahead as to what we do long term. It would be good if Julieanne could stay behind for a chat as she is the one who helps mostly with the children and will know more about the risks today. We must protect them and their parents from capture and almost certain deaths of them and probably us."

Julieanne followed Marie to her room after prayers.

"How are the children coping?" asked Marie to start off with.

"They are quite anxious, having had to hide from the Germans twice now. They are on edge and keep asking if the horrible men will come back."

Marie looked serious as she thought about what she had just heard.

"I think we must get them away from here. It was bad enough when they were restricted in where they could go so as to avoid being seen but we can't have them frightened like this. Ok I'll get on to my contact and see what can be done and sooner the better."

"What about the adults?"

"I honestly don't know. I hadn't expected this to happen so soon. I'm not naïve, I knew we would be interfered with at some point but hoped it could be put off as long as possible."

Julieanne nodded. "Do you want me to keep them in the hideaway until you have some news?"

"I think it would be for the best," said Marie, looking unhappy. She really hated doing this. What was a safe place, was now a dangerous. How she wished she knew who the traitor was and how to find out. It could be anyone.

Julieanne stood up and after the regulation curtsy left the room to go back to the children. She had a real gift for working with them which had made her the ideal choice for looking after those who came to hide from the Germans.

....

There was a banging on the door. Marie had been lost in thought and came back to earth at the noise. She got up to investigate, hoping it wasn't the Germans again although she had heard nothing.

"Belle!" cried Marie when she answered the door. "You're back. Thank God."

Belle almost fell into Marie's arms as she entered the convent. It was obvious to Marie that she'd had a terrible time. Her face, a deathly pallor, with lines of pain that hadn't been there before.

"What did they do to you?" asked Marie, sitting Belle down just inside.

Belle just shook her head, unable to answer. She lifted her top up and showed the marks that were signs of the beating she had received. Her hands were reddened from being forced into boiling water and held there.

"Come on I'm taking you to the infirmary where you can lie down and we'll examine you for other injuries. We'll probably get the doctor to come and look at you."

Hearing that Belle drew her arms protectively around herself and let out an ear splitting scream. Marie put her arm around the nun to try and reassure her. There were no words that Marie could offer that would bring consolation to Belle.

Monique, hearing the noise came hurrying along. "Belle, you're home."

Marie looked at Monique and gave a slight shake of her head, indicating that now was not the time for questions.

"Can you help me take her to the infirmary," Marie asked.

Monique quietly went to the other side and helped Marie lift the nun off the chair and walked with her. It was a slow walk as Belle was in so much pain and was bent over.

Monique made no comment but thought plenty. If only she could have five minutes with the men who did this she'd tell them what she thought of them. It was cowardly beating up a woman like that especially a nun. They should show more respect. She sighed, she knew it wouldn't make any difference. They were inhuman, savages. She knew she shouldn't feel like this. They were to be pitied and forgiven but she couldn't find forgiveness in her heart only anger.

Monique glanced at Marie and saw the set look on her face and knew she felt the same. They would have to discuss the situation later but now Belle must take priority.

They tried to lay Belle down on the bed but it was impossible as she was in so much pain that anything touching her body hurt. In fact she hurt all over. The burns were seen to and Marie sent Monique to contact the doctor.

Belle sat there shaking violently, her teeth chattering. She wasn't cold in fact she was burning up which worried Marie.

It wasn't long before the doctor arrived. He'd had a brief chat with Monique on the way in so had some idea what to expect. When he saw Belle, however, he couldn't help but be appalled at what the animals had done. His hatred of the

Germans went up a notch. He sat down and tried to have a chat with Belle to find out exactly what had happened. Belle was unable to answer. Marie filled him in on what she had seen so he had some idea of what to look at. What Marie didn't say was her fear that Belle had been raped. She didn't know how to approach it with Belle or the doctor.

The doctor though had no such qualms, he needed to know everything if he were to help.

Belle shook her head at the question the doctor posed. The Germans hadn't touched her in that way.

Marie and Monique both breathed a sigh of relief. At least they'd left her alone in that way. Belle would still take a long time to get over this physically and psychologically and being raped would have taken longer if ever.

What had this world come to that nuns were no longer respected by those outside the convent walls? But then, the Germans had no respect for anyone. They probably were suspicious of themselves wondering if each other were really loyal to Adolf Hitler and the Third Reich.

"Are you feeling up to telling us what happened?" asked Marie after the doctor had left, with promises to return the next day.

Belle shook her head, still unable to speak.

"There is an important question I need to ask? You can nod or shake your head. Were they questioning you about harbouring Jews and children?"

Belle nodded, then whispered, "This isn't the end. You need to get rid of them. The Germans say they have seen the children. It's only a matter of time before they raid us again. They believe there must be a secret hideout and will conduct a search for that."

Marie nodded with her mouth in a straight line. How she wished she knew who the traitor was. She would deal with them severely. Ideally she'd strangle them for what they had done but that was impossible.

Monique looked at Marie without a word and Marie nodded, indicating the door. They would chat outside, not in front of Belle.

Back in Marie's office Monique sat herself down comfortably in the chair opposite Marie.

"Ok I've been in touch with my contact and they are doing their best to get the Jews away. They say however, that they can't move them all at once as it would look too obvious. It would be in small groups. They weren't sure yet about the adults, but have suggested that Eve must stay here disguised as a nun as the Germans have seen her and believe her to be one of us."

Monique nodded and said, "What terrible times we live in."

"I know," said Marie giving a deep sigh. "I almost wish I hadn't become Mother Superior. The weight is all on my shoulders."

"You can always offload to me," said Monique.

"Thank you. It means a great deal that I can trust someone at least. I had hoped we would be left alone for longer so we could take in more Jews. Obviously that has to stop now, at least for the time being."

"It's sad that we can't continue but I understand the reasons why. Will we be able to start again at a later date do you think?"

Marie shook her head, "I asked the same question but it is inadvisable. The Germans won't forget this. It is just possible we'll not be able to stay either without fear of further arrests."

"What I wouldn't give to get hold of Hitler and shake him until his teeth rattled."

Marie gave a slight smile at the thought, "That's a nice thought but not something we should contemplate as nuns."

"I know," sighed Monique. "I'll have to confess it to the priest I suppose."

"Me too."

"Hey, do you think it could be Julieanne who's the one informing on us?"

"I hadn't thought of that. Yeah she knows everything since she's in charge of looking after the children. You could be right. It's certainly something for me to think about and try to look into as long as I'm subtle about it. I don't want people getting hurt when they realise what I'm accusing them of."

"I understand that but surely no one would mind as they know what is at stake here. Only the informer would dislike it."

"That's the problem if I do happen to guess on the informer they are going to pick up very quickly that I know there is a traitor in our midst."

"I hadn't thought of that. Yes, I agree, you do need to be careful then. We don't want anyone to know what we're doing."

Marie sighed, "I wish it wasn't so difficult. When I agreed to take over as Mother Superior I never imagined I'd have to take such a role during these difficult times."

"And you've done a good job of it as well. You've nothing to feel guilty over. You've come up trumps and led us according to your conscience and faith."

"Thanks for the encouragement. I just don't feel I'm doing a good job of it right now."

"You are even if you don't see it. I admire you for how well you've handled a tricky situation. You seem to know what to do at every turn."

"I really appreciate your support Monique. Now I should get back to work. Can I leave you to tell Eve that she should stay here and take the role of a nun as the Germans know her as one of us."

Monique nodded and stood up, remembering to curtsy she left the room.

Marie sat staring into space when she was on her own once again. She needed inspiration desperately. She didn't want to have any awkward interviews with potential spies. She wasn't supposed to hurt members of the community of nuns or she would lose the respect she had. She still hoped it wouldn't be any of her nuns who were giving Germans information about their activities. She had to admit though that it must be coming from someone inside the convent walls. It was disturbing and was causing many sleepless nights, unsure what would happen. It was hard living in such uncertain times under the rules of the enemy. Was it even feasible to keep the convent running under the German dictatorship? That was another thought she had to answer for the sake of them all. They looked to her for safety and it felt like too much of a responsibility. She stood up and glanced out of the window. The nuns were all going about their business as if nothing were wrong. How many of them were afraid, deeply afraid? They all appeared relaxed but how could they be when they had already been raided by the Germans twice and it could so easily happen again at any time.

Chapter Six

"Yes enter," called Marie.

"Sorry to disturb you but Belle is burning up in a fever and the doctor hasn't been in all day."

"I'm on my way," said Marie. "Could you try getting hold of the doctor for me. It does seem strange. If he says he'll come he generally does. He's very conscientious like that."

Eunice nodded.

Marie left the room hurriedly, leaving Eunice to make the call. Of course Marie realised with her out of the way Eunice could easily ring the Germans as well, but she was sure after her interview with the nun that she was innocent of the accusation that was at the forefront of Marie's mind.

Marie rushed into the infirmary and went straight to Belle. She immediately saw the reason for Eunice's worry. Belle was lying there with her eyes shut muttering to herself. Her face flushed against the white pillow. She felt Eunice's concern and hoped she'd been able to get hold of the doctor.

Eunice came back looking disturbed. The doctor wasn't there. I just got his housekeeper who said she hadn't seen him all day. He hadn't returned home for lunch which she said was unusual for him.

"Try to calm down, we can try again in a bit. He's probably been busy with urgent cases. He always comes if he says he will," said Marie, trying to calm the flustered Eunice down, although she herself was feeling anything but calm on the inside. She was desperately worried not only about Belle but the doctor as well.

"Go and get a cool flannel and wash Belle's face with it. We need to try and get her temperature down."

"Yes Mother," said Eunice rushing off to do her bidding.

Quickly returning she placed the flannel in a bowl of cold water and washed Belle with it.

"Keep doing it every five minutes or so. I'll go and try the doctor again. Even if he's out the housekeeper might have news of him."

Pleased to have something positive to do Eunice got to work. Marie left the infirmary happier in the knowledge that Eunice would nurse Belle. She was very worried over the whereabouts of the doctor however. What could have happened to him?

Back in her room she closed her eyes for a second to try to banish the worries from her mind. She felt as if she had the weight of the world on her shoulders which was not a good place to be in these times of danger when no one could be trusted.

Picking up the phone she tried the doctor again to no avail. The housekeeper still hadn't heard anything.

Not knowing what to do next Marie sat deep in thought hoping for good news soon. Surely the doctor would turn up soon apologetic for being so late. This is what Marie hoped would happen but it wasn't to be. Instead the phone rang. She picked it up on the second ring expecting to hear the doctors voice.

"Hello Reverend Mother," said the voice.

Marie recognised it as being her contact in the resistance group that helped Jews hide and eventually leave the country.

"Hello," said Marie tentatively.

"I thought I should let you know that the doctor you use whom we recommended has been taken. He was picked….."

Marie gasped. She couldn't believe what she was hearing. It couldn't be happening. They needed a doctor they could trust. Everything was going so badly wrong.

"Are you all right?" asked the voice on the end of the phone, concerned.

"Yes, it's just a shock that's all and we needed him urgently. I'm very worried about one of my nuns who was taken and interrogated Gestapo style. She is now burning up with a fever and muttering incoherently."

"I'm really sorry to hear that. At the moment I am unable to help in that way. I don't know of any other doctor I would consider safe to use. Our doctor was actually picked up as he left you yesterday. He had just got outside when the Germans took him. They took him to headquarters which is a bad sign in itself. I don't know anymore since then. Anything could have happened by now. I don't know if he is still there or if he has disappeared like so many others, never to be seen again."

"This is truly awful."

"I know. We only know this as we have been hiding watching the comings and goings from the convent. For some reason the Germans have latched onto you. They also have been observed by our people watching you. Currently it isn't safe to get rid of anyone not even the children. They would be picked up straight away then the game would be over."

"I think you use the wrong terminology there. This is no game. This is real life and a dangerous one at that."

"I know and I don't mean it like that. It strikes me as being a game of cat and mouse and we have to make sure we win. Anyway I must go before I get captured. On a final note of caution be very, very careful. Don't admit anyone you don't know. Assume everyone is a spy for the Germans and don't trust."

"This is so hard but I agree with you. I only put my trust in the Lord almighty."

"That's the best way. He can always be trusted and Our Lady will be interceding for us," said the resistance worker like the good Catholic that he was.

The phone went dead and Marie put it down thoughtfully. Things were getting very bad. Would it come to the point when they themselves needed to flee to safety with the Germans keeping the convent in their sights. Would the priest even be allowed through to hear their confession and give mass.

Marie stood up. She felt the need to go to the chapel and pray for guidance which she surely needed. She knew the doctor needed prayer as well wherever he was dead or alive.

In the chapel she crossed herself before the cross of Christ crucified and went to kneel in prayer at the altar.

"Oh Mary the mother of God....." she began. She prayed like she'd never prayed before, believing that Mary would intercede for her as she had done so many times in the past.

This time however, Marie felt no peace, only a sense of immediate danger which seemed to fill the atmosphere which was charged with electricity. The chapel had previously been a place to find peace but no more. The Germans had a lot to answer for and Marie hoped that one day the nightmare would be over and they would see them punished for the crimes they committed. Crimes against humanity, against God's chosen people, the Jews.

Marie knew she was doing the right thing by shielding the Jews. She had the responsibility as did all Christians to help in this crisis.

What would happen next, she dreaded to think. It was bad news about the doctor though. What must the poor man be thinking and feeling right now, that's if he was still alive. She felt she was to blame for his arrest. If she hadn't called him out to see Belle then he might still be safe at home. It didn't occur to her that if he hadn't been arrested then he would be another time as he worked closely with the convent people.

The door was opened. Marie turned round and smiled when she saw Monique enter. Monique crossed herself and approached her.

"What's happening?"

"Not a lot. The doctor has been arrested, he was leaving here when the Germans intercepted him and took him off."

"Oh no that's a disaster. Will he talk do you think?"

"I don't know, anything could happen. How do any of us know how we would stand up to the torture the Gestapo deal in."

"What about the Jews we need to get rid of them. They are not safe."

"I know and I posed that problem to the resistance but they said we are surrounded by Germans. It's not safe to move any one at the moment."

"This is disgraceful. You would think they would leave us alone as we are people of God."

"Maybe we still would be if we hadn't chosen to help hide Jews needing shelter."

"The Germans wouldn't know about that if someone hadn't told them. More than ever we need to find out who the collaborator is and deal with them severely."

"I think all I can do when I find out is hand the case to the resistance. I wouldn't be comfortable giving out punishment that would need to be harsh and serve a lesson to anyone else who might be contemplating showing loyalty to the Third Reich."

Monique nodded. "I'm just glad I'm not in your position."

"I would give anything not to be in this position as well," said Marie.

"You're doing a great job if that's any consolation."

"Thanks. I need your encouragement as well as God's guidance. We live in such desperate times. The last war was supposed to be the war to end all wars and look at us now, in the same position. A maniac is trying to take over the world and rid the world of God's chosen people at the same time."

"I know. We can only put our trust in God and hope He will bring us through it and bring an end to the Nazi regime which is pure evil."

Marie sighed and shook her head, not having the words to reply to Monique or to pray to Our Lady. "I don't know why I continue kneeling here as I really can't find the words to pray."

Chapter Seven

Marie picked up the phone. It was a few days after the doctor had been taken. There had been no news in all that time. She hoped every time the phone rang that it would be news one way or another. But no.

"Hello," said the voice which was barely audible.

"Who is this?" asked Marie.

"Priest," said the voice and stopped.

"Yes?"

"Sorry I won't be able to come to minister to you anymore. The Germans have warned me I face arrest and deportation if I do. They really seem to have it in for you. I don't know what's going on but you need to be very careful."

"Thank you for letting me know," said Marie. With a heartfelt sigh she put the phone down.

What more could happen? She was very scared for the whole community. They should have been safe behind their walls. Now she felt they were in grave danger.

The bell went for lunch and she got up. She was very reluctant to move, not sure what she would tell the others about the latest occurrence. She knew she had to say something though. They deserved to know the truth.

. . . .

"Listen up everyone," said Marie as they finished lunch. Her insides were turning over to the extent she had hardly eaten which had been noticeable. She was still unsure what she would say but needed them to know what was happening. They would soon be asking questions if she didn't.

The nuns, which now included Eve, looked to the end of the long table where Marie sat at the head as befitted her position as Mother Superior.

"First of all Belle is running a high fever which has us very worried for her life. The doctor hasn't been in as promised because I heard from my contact that he has been taken by the Germans."

There was a lot of talking at this news. Marie let them have their way at first, knowing they needed an outlet.

After a few minutes she held up her hand for silence. They instantly obeyed. "I'm sorry but that's not the end of the bad news. I had a phone call from our priest to say he will no longer be coming as he has been threatened. Unfortunately I don't know what our future will hold now we have come to the attention of the Germans who are keeping a close watch on our comings and goings. Any questions or concerns?"

"What about the Jews?" asked Julieanne.

"They will have to stay for the present as we are under close surveillance at the moment. It would be too dangerous to move them as they would be seen and arrested immediately as would we."

Most of the nuns were struck dumb at the news they were receiving. They were a complete blank, not knowing what to say or do.

"What do we do now?" asked Eunice.

"We carry on as normal as we can for now," said Marie. "My door is open to anyone who needs to talk or has any questions. Why don't we just spend a few minutes in prayer. Don't forget to pray for the Germans as well."

At that last sentence there was uproar which Marie had expected. She didn't know where that last sentence had come from as she also didn't want to pray for them.

"Yes, yes I know. We all need forgiveness and salvation and this includes our enemies. Most of the Germans are only following orders or they themselves will be treated brutally as well. They are human beings and are not all evil. There is good in everyone somewhere, however well hidden it may be."

There was silence while they bowed their heads in prayer asking that Mary the mother of Jesus would watch over them and keep them safe.

"Instead of the usual time of silence I think we can break that for now. You probably all have thoughts going round and round in your heads as this is a lot to take in."

Marie stood up and went on her way to her room and the solitude she craved. It wasn't to last for long though as Monique arrived. Marie wasn't surprised. She had expected her.

"Is there really nothing we can do?" asked Monique.

"Not at present no. We are surrounded by Germans. The resistance are watching from afar and what they say doesn't bode well."

"You know many of the nuns are very afraid of what may happen."

"I'm not surprised," said Marie. "I am also. It's the feeling of being trapped and not knowing how to get out of this very present danger we are all in. Whoever it is who informed on us has a lot to answer for and should be dealt with in the most severe way possible."

Monique didn't know how to respond to this. She never expected the quiet calm of her superior would reveal such hatred and anger in her voice and words. It came as a shock that Marie was hinting that the collaborator should die.

"Is there nothing at all we can do to keep ourselves safe?"

Marie shook her head. "Not anymore as we are in the sights of the enemy who will come in hard. I suspect if we tried to leave to escape their attentions we would be arrested immediately, although I'm waiting for word on that from my contact in the resistance."

"Do you regret hiding Jews and being involved? Maybe we should have kept out of it."

"We couldn't do that. I was agreeing as we have a duty from God to help His people in times of trouble and persecution. I am sure He will bless us for it."

"But He's not keeping us safe from harm is he," said Monique with a hint of bitterness in her voice.

"You don't think we did the right thing by taking them in."

"I did at the time but now I'm not so sure. It has put us in grave danger and who knows when or how it will end."

"I do understand your feelings. I went into it with my eyes open but still I believe we did the right thing. Just think how many Jews we have rescued and sent them on their way to the freedom of England eventually. We can just hope they all made it to safety, but that we'll never know."

"I know this may seem strange but is it possible it's someone from the resistance themselves who told on us."

"I hadn't thought of that. I will mention it to my contact."

"You never mention him by name. That seems strange."

"I've been told not to admit where my source comes from. It could put him and the rest of this resistance group in danger if the Germans knew of names. It's on a need to know basis only. I've never met him, I just know his voice over the telephone and it's probable that it's disguised as he always sounds a bit funny if you know what I mean."

"Yeah I think I understand."

"Good. Do you feel a bit better now we've had this conversation and you've had a chance to air your feelings and understand why I've taken the action we have. I don't regret it for one minute. I still believe we did the right thing. I suppose we were lucky that we were able to carry on for this long without the Germans becoming suspicious."

"You're right. You still have my full support."

"Thank you," said Marie, allowing her face to relax into a bit of a smile.

Monique bobbed the usual curtsy and left the room, leaving Marie to her own thoughts. Although Marie had tried to sound positive and sure of herself to Monique, inside she wasn't as certain that she had done the right thing by sheltering Jews. Yes, at the start she had known there would be danger involved but she wasn't at all sure she had totally understood the repercussions for the community as a whole. She felt guilty for putting them all in danger as they now were. Inside she felt only fear, not just for herself but for the other nuns. It was through her actions that they were now in this position. Her responsibility. It was her fault that Belle had been so badly hurt at the hands of the Germans and if she were to die it would be Marie with blood on her hands. She really didn't like this responsibility. Maybe she wasn't cut out to lead them as she led them all into danger. Thinking about it in hindsight she wasn't convinced she had thought it through properly. Would she have done the same thing if she had really understood the evil of Nazism and what it would lead to?

It had been just before the invasion by the Germans that she had been approached about hiding the Jews. Maybe she had been a bit naïve and thought it was all a bit melodramatic. She knew with certainty that she had never believed that they would over run her country. She had believed the British would never allow it, but they had been forced to retreat to Dunkirk and leave for England again. The Germans had control of France and they had no mercy on the French people. She had heard all about the reprisals if any act of resistance took place. It had become quite normal for people to be taken and publicly shot. Even living apart in the convent such news filtered in through their walls.

Chapter Eight

"Please come quick," said Eunice, rushing into Marie's room and interrupting her reverie.

Not needing to hear anymore Marie stood up and followed Eunice out of the room. She followed Eunice up to the infirmary where she found Belle worse. The mutterings were getting louder and the flushed face told Marie everything she needed to know. Even though she wasn't a qualified nurse as Eunice was she could see for herself that Belle was very bad. She knew she would blame herself if anything happened to Belle and it really didn't look good right now. Eunice had uncovered her and exposed the sores which were now weeping and full of pus. Belle clearly had a severe infection set into her wounds.

"Have you tried using salt water on them, it might help and in the absence of a doctor is all we have at our disposal."

"I have yes and will continue to do so every hour."

Marie nodded.

Marie glanced at Eunice who shook her head. Belle appeared to be unconscious but Eunice didn't want to take any chances that Belle might hear and understand. Eunice felt it was just a matter of time before Belle lost her slim hold on life.

Tears glistened in Marie's eyes which Eunice saw. She took of her Marie's hand in a gesture of comfort and reassurance.

"It's not your fault," said Eunice quietly.

Marie shook her head in denial. She knew it was very much her fault. She really had the weight of the world on her shoulders right now and she felt she had made some very poor decisions.

"It's all of us," said Eunice. "We supported your decision to help the Jews. It seemed the right thing to do at the time and I don't have any regrets at all."

"But it was my duty to protect you and I failed."

"We all went into this with our eyes open. Anyway, if we hadn't helped the Jews we would still have come to the attention of the Nazis eventually. They would have attacked us for our religious beliefs. You did the right thing. Belle wouldn't want you to blame yourself. She fully supported you and was quite vocal about it even when it started to go wrong when the Germans first came and searched."

Marie nodded but didn't believe it for now. She would give anything to see Belle up and about and full of life as usual. She would even excuse her talking when they were supposed to be in silence as she had always done. Belle had certainly been a live wire who couldn't keep quiet. Even with that fault she was still popular with Marie, as she was hard working and caring by nature. If she didn't survive and Marie was in no doubt that she was fighting for her life right now, then Marie would never forgive herself. She knew deep down that the Germans could have pounced on them for any little thing but this in her mind was all her fault for the decisions she made about the Jews.

"Look, I think you should have a break Eunice, I'll sit with Belle for now."

"Well ok if you're sure. I won't be long though but yes a break would be much appreciated."

Eunice left the infirmary to face questions from the others. Not wanting to answer each nun individually she decided to tell them all at once. When they were all gathered around her she spoke, telling them the situation without sugar coating it. They needed to know and prepare for the worst right now. Although the nuns had no particular friendships they all cared deeply about each other. They were one big happy family most of the time. Hiding the Jews had been part of their job as nuns. Surely no one could really standby and let the Germans destroy a whole race which would happen if they had their way. They were truly evil doing the devils work, committing terrible atrocities.

....

"How is she now?" asked Eunice arriving back in the infirmary after a while.

Marie shrugged which Eunice took to mean as about the same. She longed to see improvement but knew the reality was that they would lose Belle and sooner rather than later, probably within the next hour or two.

"I don't like that fever," said Marie. "I'm sure it's gone up a notch or two."

Eunice got the thermometer and took the necessary temperature. Sure enough it was slightly raised which indicated some sort of infection which they were already aware of.

Marie's face was set firm looking very serious with her pursed lips, tightly pressed together. Five minutes with the Germans who did this had much to answer for and she'd give them what for. They would be taken by surprise if it came from a woman but someone needed to do something. Inside she knew she couldn't as she would be shot straight away and there could be further reprisals on the nuns. She sighed. What had this world come to? It was a dangerous place to live. All she could realistically do was pray for God to intervene but nothing happened. It was as if she was praying into a void. She knew she was in danger of losing her faith and she didn't want that to happen or she knew she would be condemned to hell which would deliver torture worse than the Germans could even think of and that was saying something.

At that moment there was a groan from the bed, which interrupted Marie's thoughts, probably for the best.

Marie and Eunice both leaned forward. Belle had her eyes open staring into space as if she was somewhere else entirely. Her eyes were bright, glistening full of fever as she continued rambling incoherently.

Marie noticed there were little spots appearing on Belle's usually unblemished skin. She pointed it out to Eunice who saw and looked extremely serious. This was the end they both knew it. The infection had got into the bloodstream. Eunice indicated to Marie to move away from the bed as she wanted a word.

"Do you want me to let the others know so they can come and say goodbye?"

"I'm not sure as it would be very distressing and some of the nuns are quite highly strung. I don't want to give everyone nightmares."

"Understood. I just thought it might be for the best as she appears to have very……"

Eunice was interrupted by a loud sigh from the bed which in fact was Belle struggling to take a breath as her body was ravaged by the infection.

Marie and Eunice rushed to the bed and Marie said, "It's ok Belle, we're here with you. You can go on to the next life when you're ready."

Belle opened her eyes briefly and gave a small smile and that was it. With tears in her eyes Marie closed Belle's eyes for the final time.

Both Marie's and Eunice's eyes filled up and spilled out and down their face, running freely. Neither spoke. What was there to say? Marie was glad she had been there at the end. It was probably no comfort to Belle who had been unconscious, possibly unaware of anyone being present. It had at least been able to give comfort to Marie and Eunice who witnessed the end and were able to gain some peace that Belle's suffering was over.

Marie couldn't help wondering if the outcome would have been different if the doctor had turned up as expected. Possibly not.

Marie was angry inside and wished she could punch something or someone. Belle had been refused the last rites which had been the job of the priest but with him refusing to come and serve them anymore it hadn't happened. Whoever had informed on them had a lot to answer for and had one death on their conscience so far, and who knows how many more before this ended.

"I better go and tell the others, they'll want to know what has happened," said Marie, standing up.

Eunice nodded and said, "I'll see to Belle so don't worry about that. Where will we bury her? I assume the priest will refuse to take the service."

"I have no idea what we can do at the moment. I'll have to get in touch with my contact and see what they can suggest. We may have to bury her in the grounds here to try and keep away from the Germans noticing what has happened."

"Do you think they would show any remorse for what they've done?"

"I doubt it. They seem devoid of any feeling for their fellow humans. You just have to see what they are doing to the Jews to know that."

Eunice nodded, "I know you're right but somewhere deep inside I had hope that there is some good in the German people."

"I'm sure there are in the population as a whole but I doubt there is in the Nazi party amongst the SS and the Gestapo."

....

It was a chilly day when the funeral was held. The ground was hard but somehow they had managed to dig the necessary hole for the burial. The rest of the nuns had been stunned into silence since hearing the news of Belle's death. They all stood outside in silence. Many were hugging themselves in an effort to keep warm and to find comfort as shaken as they were by the recent events.

Belle was joining those who had passed before in the convent. She would never be forgotten by those still living, known as she would be as a victim of the cruel Nazi regime.

Chapter Nine

Nothing more had happened since Belle's death. Marie was in regular contact with the resistance but no more news had been heard. The Germans still kept up their watch outside the convent walls but they made no attempt to interfere with the nuns. Marie wasn't deceived though, she knew they would be paying close attention to what was happening and would pounce at the slightest suspicion. She thanked God at the end of each day that they had no more searches and were semi safe, at least for the moment.

The nuns, still shocked by recent events went about their business like robots. Even during recreation when they could talk quietly they were silent, unable to voice their thoughts.

Marie felt this was unhealthy but her attempts at getting them to talk about what had happened led nowhere. No one wanted to speak. Even in the privacy of her room no one spoke, not even Monique who so regularly visited Marie. It was as if Belle was being swept under the carpet, forgotten. It wasn't like that though as many cried in the privacy of their rooms. The religious life didn't give much time for the bearing of emotions but Marie felt that had to change to suit the challenging times they lived in. Violence was not the norm previously and being shut off from the outside world to all intents and purposes they didn't get much news of what was happening in the outside their walls. They were no longer shut out and had regular updates from the resistance which Marie always passed on so everyone knew what was happening.

This wasn't done to spread fear amongst the women but to inform them so they could pray about the desperate state of the world.

The Jews still resided in the convent but remained hidden. To all intents and purposes there were no Jews and that was how it had to remain. The constant presence of the Germans outside meant there was no safe way to move them. Eve fully embraced the convent life as if she were a fully fledged nun. At first she felt uncomfortable but as time had gone on it became the norm. She was allowed time to spend with her daughter and relished it as precious. Francesca was growing fast. She wasn't the innocent girl she had once been though. She was sombre and quiet. She'd had to grow up quickly as had all the Jewish children being hidden.

It upset Marie to see how quiet and obedient they were. Accepting of their fate almost. They should be running around, playing happily and getting into mischief as all young children should. They were safe – at least for the moment. That was the main thing. The convent was once more seen as a place of safety by those inside it. At times they were able to ignore the threatening presence outside and pretend everything was as it should be.

They still had no doctor if any of the nuns or Jews were to become ill. The doctor had been released after a month inside going through who knows what. He was back home now convalescing but he refused to go anymore to minister to the nuns where they had need. The resistance were unwilling to introduce another doctor to them, not being sure who would be safe.

The lack of priest was still someone greatly missed. Marie did her best to hold Sunday services but they had no mass. Marie, at first had tried herself to hear confession but it hadn't worked as the nuns felt too self conscious to say anything to their leader as respected as much as she was.

It was a major disruption of their routine but it couldn't be helped and maybe was safer even. With no one coming in for any reason there was no one to inform on them. It still left the question in the minds of some of the nuns over who it could be. Marie and Monique were sure it must be a nun but the lack of further raids made them doubt it. It was a very strange state of affairs because surely if it was someone from outside, such as the doctor or priest, they would have continued visiting to get more information to pass on.

....

"Y'know I find it strange that no one has informed on us since Eve and Belle were taken. We still have the Jews here which all know about," said Marie to Monique during one of their recent chats.

"Maybe we finally convinced them," replied Monique.

"I doubt it. They wouldn't be sat outside watching if they believed us."

"True," said Monique with a heavy sigh.

"What's on your mind?"

"I dunno. It just seems odd. Nothing has changed so there really is no need for the collaborator to stop."

"I agree. I can't stop thinking that they are playing some game with us. Maybe to lull us into a false sense of security and make us take up work with the resistance group again," said Marie.

"You could be right."

"I just wish I knew who it is and what they are up to. I find myself looking around and wondering if it could be that person or another."

"I, too, am suspicious of everyone. How sad it is that we live in such times that means no one can be trusted. We should be able to trust each other to live side by side as we do, observing the religious life. What would our Lady say about it I wonder," said Monique.

"I suppose we shouldn't be trusting each other as it could easily be one of us."

"I know but if we don't trust each other we'll trust no one and then we're in trouble. We'd have to keep everything to ourselves which would do us no good at all."

On that note there was a knock on the door and Eunice entered.

"Yes what is it?" asked Marie formally.

"It's the children they are getting fractious being cooped up for so long. They need to be outside running around."

"I'm sorry, I understand how they must feel but it's too dangerous for them and us if they were to be allowed out."

Eunice sighed before saying, "I thought you'd say that but I promised Julieanne that I'd mention it to you."

Monique gave Marie a look which was returned before Marie said, "Tell her it's not safe and there is nothing we can do about it at present."

When Eunice had gone, Monique said, "That's interesting. Why would Julieanne be so keen to get the children outside when she knows as well as we all do that it isn't safe for the Jews to be outside at all. Of course the children need to be out in the fresh air but it's not possible."

Marie nodded. "I agree and it certainly sounds fishy to me as well. My first thought was that maybe she is the informer and she's trying to move things on a bit."

Monique agreed and said so.

"How can we find out?" asked Monique.

"I'm not sure at the moment," said Marie. "I'll have to think of a subtle way to do it."

"Rather you than me, I'm not exactly known for my tact and subtlety," said Monique.

Marie laughed and said, "That's very true. Maybe that's why I'm in charge here and not you. You wouldn't be a good choice. You'd be upsetting everyone and the whole convent would be an uproar instead of the peaceful, calm place it's meant to be."

Monique laughed as well. She bore no malice towards Marie for stating the truth. She knew herself well and her strengths and weaknesses and she was no leadership material.

Again there was a knock on the door. Eunice entered. "Sorry to bother you again but a fight has broken out amongst the children. That new child Francesca is in the middle of it and is in danger of getting hurt."

"Can't Juliette deal with it? She's supposed to be in charge of the children," responded Marie.

Eunice shook her head.

Marie stood up reluctantly, "Well I'd better come and see what's happening I suppose."

Marie followed Eunice along the corridor and into the kitchen where they pressed a small button which revealed a door behind a wall which they entered. It was a long, dark tunnel. Eunice switched on her torch so they could see where they were going. The tunnel led downwards into a basement. They could hear nothing as they walked. It was well sealed and insulated so no would could hear anything. The resistance had arranged it all when they had approached them about helping with the Jews before the invasion. They were preparing for the inevitable and Marie was now thankful for it because it was coming to good use.

They came to the end where a sturdy door stood shut. Giving three knocks they waited for Julieanne to come and let them in. This was a signal that it was other nuns and perfectly safe for Julieanne to approach. The door couldn't be opened from the other side in the tunnel only someone in the basement could open it.

Sure enough Julieanne didn't leave them waiting long which Marie was thankful for considering the cold, damp feel of the tunnel.

Marie and Eunice entered and looked around assessing the situation.

"Well everything seems ok now," said Marie, slightly annoyed at having to go there for nothing.

"Sorry Mother, they only settled down shortly before you knocked on the door."

Marie said nothing but pursed her lips. She glanced around at the pale faces anxiously watching her. "It's ok children. Nothing to worry about. Is everyone ok?" she asked in an effort to reassure them as much as to obtain any information as to what had just occurred.

"Is anyone hurt?" asked Eunice.

"No," chorused the children.

Marie looked at Julieanne and saw the flushed face of embarrassment. She wondered just what had been going on. Had she been called there deliberately as a ruse. Was something else occurring in another part of the building that necessitated getting Marie out of the way. Marie couldn't help being a bit suspicious.

"Well seeing everything is fine down here I won't keep you. You should get back to the children."

Marie turned her back and left the basement to make her way back up the tunnel. She stopped halfway, breathless and legs aching. She really wasn't as fit as she could be she realised. She hoped she could get out and get some real exercise soon. She used to be fitter than this. She couldn't believe how out of shape she had become.

Continuing on her way up she suddenly paused. Turning around to Eunice she put a finger to her lips to ensure Eunice kept quiet. Eunice raised her eyebrows querying Marie. Marie shook her head but said nothing. She indicated they turn around and go back to the basement. Seeing nothing for it but to obey she followed Marie back down and knocked on the door again.

"Who is it?" called Julieanne.

"Us," said Marie.

Opening the door wide for them to enter Julieanne looked quite surprised to see them and raised her eyebrows.

When the door was shut Marie said, "I heard male voices coming from above. I was worried it was the Germans again so thought it better to come down and wait it out here.

"I understand," said Eunice. "We can't risk them suddenly seeing us."

Marie went and sat on an empty space on a bench set along the side of the room.

"We were just playing Chinese whispers weren't we children," said Julieanne.

The children nodded eagerly. They loved that game, even the older ones. They never knew what the story would be when they finished getting to the end of the line. There were about twenty children there at that time which was the most they had ever had. This gave plenty of scope for the original story to be changed many times. It gave them all a good laugh to hear the final version of the story.

Sometimes their play had taken on an educational role to try and prevent them from becoming too behind when they were attending school again which the adults hoped would be very soon although the way things were outside it didn't look as if it would be yet.

Marie sometimes wondered if the norm would ever happen again. She would give anything for the sometimes boring routine of convent life. She didn't relish the drama they now lived. Not knowing what would happen next and if there would be any more casualties of this war to join Belle. At least that meant that Belle wasn't the informer.

Eunice and Marie stayed in the basement playing games with the children for a good hour before Marie deemed it safe to leave.

Following the same route back they were quiet, straining their ears for any sounds from above except the normal ones.

All was quiet so they made it into the kitchen where they found the place in an uproar. It seemed Marie had been right the Germans had been and turned the place upside down. Everything was a mess. At a quick glance Marie realised it would take a lot of work to restore order to the life of the nuns.

Marie went straight to her room to see if she could get hold of her contact to see what he knew of these events.

"Someone informed on you again. They were looking for a secret entrance going to a hidden room which was full of Jewish children," said Jacque the resistance worker gravely.

"Who would do such a thing? These are only innocent children, some still very young. They are no threat to anyone."

"I know. We have to rethink things because the chances are the Germans will be back sooner rather than later. I wouldn't put it passed them to completely trash the place determined to find the secret room. You are all in great danger, not just the Jews this time. The Germans are on a mission and have it in for you it seems."

"What can we do though?"

"We need somewhere to hide the children and adults for some time until we can be sure it's safe again. Have you anywhere in your grounds that would be safer than the hidden basement?"

"I don't know. The chapel might work but it will be a bit of a squash going in the room behind the oak panelling. It's only a storeroom of sorts where we keep the holy sacrament."

"Look, I'll have a think and get back to you as soon as I can."

"Thank you," said Marie who sat still and quiet. Shoulders slumped as if she had the weight of the world on her shoulders, which she felt she did at that moment.

What were they to do? If only she knew who it was who was informing on them. That way they could be dealt with in the severest possible way. Marie knew now that she would hand the collaborator over to the resistance who would do the deed. They were going too far by giving up the children to the Germans. It was bad enough when it was the adults but to target young children was below the belt in every way.

Monique knocked and entered, looking shaken she said, "I don't know how much more I can take after today's activities."

"I know how you feel. Although I wasn't around. I had been called away to the children who were supposedly fighting. When I got there they were absolutely fine. I think it was a ruse to get me away from the search. Someone decided I was at risk and wanted me gone for some reason. I wish I knew who it was though."

"If it was a problem with the children could it mean it was Julieanne. If she had known when the raid was to take place she could have sent that message."

"That's what I thought but decided it didn't make sense. Get me away yes, but how could she then get to the phone to inform on us again. She couldn't have left the basement and there is no connection down there."

"I hadn't thought of that."

"Neither had I until I was seriously considering it could be her. Is there much damage? I only saw the state of the kitchen and came straight here."

"A lot I'm afraid. They have broken things and ripped up bedding. They have left us with a lot of work to do if we are to stay here."

"You think we should leave?" asked Marie, who had been thinking along the same lines.

"Yes, I seriously think we need to consider it. No one is safe here."

"But if we leave we could all be picked up by the Germans. What would we do with the Jews. We couldn't safely take them with us could we. The only other option as I see it is to let a few of the Jews go under cover of darkness and see what happens."

"The problem being we don't want news of what we are doing to be broadcast outside you and me and your contact or the information could get into the wrong hands."

"Unless we broadcast an inaccurate message to a few nuns and see what happens. That way we could eliminate people from the list of possible informers."

"Sounds a good plan," said Monique. "I propose you try a message with Julieanne since she has to be top of the list of suspects at this present moment.

"I'll talk it over when Jacques gets in touch. It's a possibility. We can't leave things as they are. We must take action that is appropriate because of the growing danger we and the Jews are in."

Chapter Ten

"Monique would you mind passing a message to Julieanne and tell her it's in the strictest confidence please. Tell her that we will be moving some of the Jews tonight undercover of darkness."

"You've had some news then?"

"Not really just the go ahead to try and trap the collaborator. Jacque has agreed to deal with the person when we are sure we know who it is."

"You still think it could be Julieanne?"

"Yes," replied Marie. "At least she's a starting point."

"Do you want me to send her to you?"

Marie shook her head. "No I want her to stay down there where it will be extremely difficult to pass on the news. I'm giving her a chance to redeem herself and ignore it."

"If it's her she might find a reason to leave the basement and get to the phone."

"I really hope it isn't her. I still wish it was someone on the outside. I don't like to think it is one of our own but it's not looking hopeful now we don't have a doctor or a priest coming in at all."

"Anyway, I better get going if I am to deliver that message in time for her to make contact with the Germans."

Marie sat back lost in thought. She hated the idea of Julieanne being the traitor. She thought back to what she knew of the nun. Not much actually which was unusual. She had very little information about her past life only that she was originally from Paris. She had come late to the convent, having done nursing first. She said she had felt the call for a few years but had ignored it at first until the call had got louder over time. She had been part of the convent since early 1939. She appeared to have no family living and Marie had observed her as being a bit of a loner within the convent walls.

The more Marie thought about it, the more it seemed likely that Julieanne was the one. That should mean once she had been dealt with they could all breathe a sigh of relief. They would hopefully be safe.

Monique delivered the message to a surprised Julieanne who hadn't expected to hear anything. She wasn't usually privy to confidential information so this came as a shock. She agreed to keep it quiet and not to tell anyone.

……..

Marie was going to make it obvious where the secret room in the chapel was to hopefully put the Germans off the scent and make it look as if they were prepared to cooperate. If they were to be seen to help it was possible the Germans would think they had nothing to hide after all. That was the best outcome for all concerned.

Of course, it was to be hoped the Germans didn't turn up in response to a message received from the convent. It would mean Julieanne wasn't the traitor. Marie was certain by this time, although happy to be proved wrong. It would be good to be wrong but it would mean going through the same process with each nun until they found who it was.

………

It was just starting to get dark when there was a lot of noise outside. Marie looked out of her window and became grim when she realised the Germans were on the doorstep. It looked as if they weren't bothering to ring the bell this time. She stood up to greet them as her door was suddenly flung open.

"Hello again, how can I help you this time?"

"We have information that Jews will be leaving here sometime tonight."

Marie looked shocked. "What Jews? I keep telling you we know nothing of any Jews here. We are a Catholic convent and go about our business quietly. We don't want any trouble."

"Well, while there are Jews here you have trouble."

"Have you found any evidence? You have been badly misinformed."

"I suspect you of not telling the truth. We have it on good authority that you've been taking in Jews before we took over your lovely country. If you don't give them up we'll have to start showing you we mean what we say."

Marie shook her head. "I can't make you believe us but you can search the place we have nothing to hide."

"You will come with us."

Marie was forced out of the room and pushed ahead of the Germans where they shoved her roughly. She passed the recreation room where all the other nuns were congregated in fear. She led their captors around the convent in every nook and cranny trying to prove the lack of Jews in the place. She even showed them the secret space in the chapel which the Germans hadn't seen before. Much to their disappointment there was no further they could go into the secret room and no Jews were found.

"You show us where they are hidden or you'll be sorry."

"I'm very sorry but I know nothing of these so called Jews. Look we have done nothing but cooperate, yet you still harass us."

"We take these allegations of Jews on these premises seriously."

Marie shook her head. "There is nothing more I can do. If you don't believe me take me away."

"I think we will get nothing more from you so we'll interrogate the other nuns living here."

Marie was taken back to the recreation room where she was roughly pushed towards the others. If she hadn't been caught by Monique she would have fallen over.

Monique was pulled out ahead of everyone else and pushed out of the room. Monique looked down at the ground, determined not to let the Germans see her fear. She wasn't the only one, many were also looking down not wanting to look the

Germans in the eye. They all realised this was serious. The Germans were wanting to make an example of them. No one knew if they would even survive this night.

Eve made eye contact with Marie who gave a slight shake of the head. She had understood the look from Eve who was suggesting she own up to being a Jew and let the Germans think they had what they'd been looking for. Eve would gladly give herself up despite her fear if it would keep the convent free of trouble and all the other Jews free and safely hidden away here.

Monique was taken back pale faced, but on her feet at least. They grabbed the next one who happened to be Eunice. She left the room head held high. She wouldn't give up any information she had whatever the Germans did to her.

Nun after nun was dragged off but gave nothing away. The Germans were becoming more angry as they dealt with each nun the same way.

"This is a waste of time. No one is going to give us what we're looking for. If we can't persuade you to talk I'll speak to the Gestapo. No one will be able to avoid their methods."

Some of the nuns were visibly shaking at this. One or two looked over at Eve wishing she would own up to being a Jew in the midst of them. Maybe if they got rid of her then the Germans might leave the rest of them alone.

It was Eunice who stepped forward. "You can take me. I'm a Jew being hidden here but to my knowledge there are no other Jews on these premises."

Marie stepped forward wanting to stop Eunice from going to a certain death, but the Germans pushed her back.

Some of the other nuns gasped but admiring of Eunice's bravery. Something no one else had the courage to say. Eunice was dragged off while the other nuns were left behind pale faced and looking toward Marie for guidance.

"Ok everyone, we have just been through a difficult time and if I'm any judge things will get worse for us. I will speak to my contact and see what he has to say. The rest of you stay here and await news which I will bring to you as soon as I know anything."

Marie left the room purposefully walked to her room where she picked up the phone. Before she could speak to the operator the phone rung and Marie answered it, not surprised to find it was Jacques.

"We have a real problem here," said Marie.

"I know, that's why I'm ringing. Your nun has just been escorted to Gestapo headquarters. Don't expect her back. They have really got it in for you. I really think you need to get the Jews and yourselves out of there as soon as we can arrange it."

"But how?"

"I really don't know, but it's your only chance at remaining alive."

"What do we do about Julieanne?" asked Marie.

"We'll deal with her very shortly have no worries about that. Send her out on some pretext and we'll take it from there."

"I really wish it hadn't come to this," said Marie sadly.

"I know. We always knew though that it must be someone on the inside. You can speak to her first to make sure there is no mistake and we have the right person."

"It must be as no one else knew except Monique who gave her the message and I trust Monique implicitly."

"I'll make some excuse to send her out after I've spoken to her."

The phone call was terminated. The call had already taken longer than usual which also carried the danger of the Germans intercepting it and knowing the full content of the conversation.

Marie went back to the room to find some of the nuns in tears, frightened by what was happening.

"We and the Jews have to leave here," she said abruptly. "When I have more news I'll let you know how we're to do this. In the meantime Julieanne can you come with me please."

Julieanne, startled stood up and followed Marie out of the room.

In her office Marie sat down but didn't invite Julieanne to sit. She faced the nun and decided to say what had to be said bluntly. There was no point going around in circles but just to come out with it.

"I believe you are the spy from within. You were the only one who knew the Jews were going to leave tonight."

Julieanne gasped, "But it wasn't me. I haven't done anything wrong. I wouldn't do that. Someone must have overheard and done it."

"It would be helpful if you could tell the truth and explain why you did it."

"I haven't done anything wrong," said Julieanne very frightened now. She could guess at the outcome if she couldn't get Marie to believe her.

Unfortunately for Julieanne, Marie was certain she had the one who was betraying them all.

"You have been with us the least time and we hardly know anything about your background. It seems clear to me. I would trust the others with my life."

"What about Eve? She has only just arrived and at the time the Germans started to visit us."

"She's a Jew seeking sanctuary here. She thought she'd be safe here but it seems not."

"How do you know she's really a Jew. She could just be saying that."

"She has a daughter she wouldn't risk her life like this."

"Can you be really sure Francesca is her daughter. She might have been planted with Eve to make her story more feasible and you've fallen for it."

Marie shook her head sadly. "I'm sorry you feel you can't be honest with me and seek absolution for your sins."

"I tell you I'm innocent," said Julieanne with a note of desperation in her voice.

"Please I need to think, go outside to the hen house and collect any eggs that are there."

Julieanne left the room in tears. She knew what would happen and sure enough as soon as she was outside and moving towards the hen house two shots rang out. Marie shook her head and tears slid down her face as she heard the shots. She was sorry it had come to this but hopefully they would be safe for now. There was still a part of Marie who wished she could have been wrong, but she was certain she was right. Her biggest regret was that Julieanne hadn't admitted to it. With a big sigh she stood up and went back to the others to let them know what had just taken place.

The nuns were all in turmoil when she reached them, having heard the shots ring out.

"Quieten down," she said and waited for them to do so before she continued, "I am sorry to say but Julieanne was a spy planted in our midst. She has now been dealt with by the resistance and hopefully we will have no more problems. I can't state enough how dangerous this is for all concerned. If you give information to the Germans or speak to someone you think is trustworthy this is the possible outcome. We live in dangerous times and can only pray that God will deliver us from this evil which has overtaken our country. Let us go to the chapel and get on our knees and pray for our Lady to intercede on Julieanne's behalf that God may forgive her and receive her into his kingdom."

The nuns all stood and followed Marie to the chapel in silence, completely stunned by what had just happened. They were looking around at each other wondering if they could be trusted. Marie realised this but left them to it. It would be better for them to be suspicious of each other. It would prevent any more information leaking out and getting to the ears of the Germans.

The nuns knelt before the cross while Marie implored the virgin Mary to intercede for them and have mercy on Julieanne. It could be said that many were not concentrating on the prayers but were thinking it could be them next. They found it very difficult to accept that one of them could have betrayed them in this way. Had Julieanne known what she was doing and done it deliberately or was she mistaken and trusted the wrong person. If the latter were the case then there was still danger in their midst. A traitor more deadly than someone making a mistake. An innocent one.

It was a very subdued set of nuns who sat down for their evening meal. Usually conversation was allowed but today no one said a word, all wondering who could be trusted.

Marie realised this could be for the best if it were to teach them all to be careful who they spoke to, even an innocent remark could be misconstrued and get into the wrong hands. She determined to have a quiet word with Eve who was just sitting there moving her knife and fork around the plate but eating nothing.

When they finished Marie touched Eve on the arm and beckoned her to follow her to her room. When they were both seated Marie said, "What's on your mind Eve? I can see something is for you hardly ate anything."

Eve stayed silent, not sure what to say what she was thinking.

"It's ok you won't get into trouble you can trust me."

"It's just that it might be better if I were to leave. I put you in danger by being here in the first place. I'm one of those they are looking for. I should just give myself up."

"No, no you must not do that. You are welcome here for as long as you need to be. Yes the situation isn't ideal but of necessity. I don't want to hear anymore talk of giving yourself up."

"But I'm not one of you. I'm a Jew and as such an enemy of the Reich."

"You came to us believing this was a place of safety and as far as I can keep you safe I will. It's easier to have you disguised as a nun. I'm sorry I've had to do that as it must be uncomfortable to pretend to share our faith."

"It feels a bit weird but I'm getting used to it now. It's almost as if I believed as you do. I have mostly learned the words you chant in the chapel so I don't look so out of place."

"Well done. You have done well in a very short space of time. Now off you go and no more worrying. Do you understand you are one of us until it is safe for you to be Jewish again, or until we leave this place whichever comes first."

Eve nodded but said nothing. In some ways she felt it was a privilege to be counted as a nun but in other ways she felt guilty, as if she was deserting her own faith. More and more she felt drawn in to the faith she was masquerading. How much longer would this state of affairs last she wondered. There was no sign of things ending any time soon.

Chapter Eleven

Next morning the nuns were still very quiet. Many were looking tired as if they hadn't slept at all with purple shadows under their eyes. Marie noticed and felt sad that this was the case. She herself had been awake tossing and turning all night wondering if she had done the right thing letting Julieanne go to her death as she did. She had it on her conscience and wondered if Julieanne would have changed if given another chance. Maybe knowing she had been found out was all that was needed. Now there was no going back, death was final. There was also an element of doubt in Marie's mind. What if Julieanne had been telling the truth and she wasn't the traitor. It would be innocent blood that would have been shed with the real traitor still around feeling thankful for the mistake. On the other hand, it was also possible that Julieanne's death would be held as an example to them all and hopefully prevent anyone else who might think of betraying them from doing so. Marie sincerely hoped there would be no more deaths amongst them.

Eunice was still on Marie's conscience. She had stood up in Eve's place and chosen to sacrifice herself to save someone in trouble. It was admirable but unnecessary. Their story had to be strong and remain consistent, that there were no Jews hiding in the convent. She knew that the resistance would do their best to find out what was happening to Eunice and would let her know when they could. She knew the likelihood of never seeing Eunice again was strong.

The nuns were very quiet all day. They went about their duties but weren't concentrating on them. Like Marie their thoughts were elsewhere.

Marie resolved to try and find out what was happening to Eunice if she continued to hear nothing. It probably meant Jacques hadn't been able to get any information. He had to be so careful himself so may have had to hide away from the Germans. If they were to ever find out his connection with the convent then he would disappear never to be heard from again. The other option would be that he would be publicly killed as an example of what would happen if anyone dared cross a German.

Marie went to bed that night but was unable to sleep. She tossed and turned with troubling thoughts going through her mind. When she did fall asleep it was full of disturbing dreams. Julieanne and Eunice just would not leave her. They were haunting her even in her sleep.

Chapter Twelve

"Hello it's Jacque speaking."

"Hello have you found out anything?" asked Marie.

"Unfortunately Eunice was put in one of the cattle trucks bound for who knows where. At least she wasn't killed."

"She might as well have been. We know no one ever returns from one of those camps that we've heard about."

"It's her own fault from what you tell me. She stood up and said she was a Jew. We know that's asking for trouble in these difficult times."

"I admire her bravery. The Germans were so certain one of us was a Jew in hiding. Who knows what would have happened if Eunice hadn't taken a stand."

"Don't forget you do have a Jew masquerading as a nun. She could have owned up."

"How could you say that! It was you who persuaded us to start hiding Jews. You said we were in the ideal position as the Germans would never realise a convent could be hiding anyone."

"I know and we have managed to keep our activities quiet until now. I just hope we were right in that Julieanne was the traitor."

"If we were wrong well....."

"I just hope to God we weren't."

"Could we still be in the Germans sights now they have become interested in us? It strikes me they have heard enough to remain suspicious then we'll never know if we still have a traitor here."

"Yes it could happen like that unfortunately. The sooner we move the Jews the better but it won't happen for that nun. If she were to disappear the Germans would definitely notice and that would be it. She will have to remain at the convent as long as you continue to exist which is not guaranteed."

Marie sighed. She hated all of this. Life was so much simpler before the Germans. She didn't regret helping the Jews. She knew that God would want them to do so. They were His chosen people. Life had become so difficult and it frightened her as to what would happen to the other nuns. They were her responsibility and in these dangerous times she found that very hard. She couldn't guarantee their survival. Nazism was truly evil and was spreading its hatred everywhere.

"I'm going to have to go now," said Jacque and disconnected the call without letting Marie respond.

What she didn't know was that Jacque was being watched by a German, a member of the hated Gestapo if he wasn't mistaken. He had noticed for a while that he was being followed but had no proof. He hoped he had been careful enough and covered his tracks well. He really needed to sort out his resistance group and get a deputy in place should anything happen to him.

Jacque hurried away but every now and again he realised he was being watched by the same man. If it hadn't been the Gestapo he might have asked what they wanted but didn't dare approach this one, he would probably end up being arrested just for talking to the wrong person.

The last thing he wanted was to be arrested and questioned. This would most likely mean torture and who knew what information would be given away under those conditions. He really needed to go to ground for a while. If he were to alert his group they could do the work whilst he hid away. What needed to happen with some urgency was to remove the Jews from the convent so that they were seen as squeaky clean. He could organise that then go into hiding. Of course this would mean letting London know he was being watched as he was actually sent by them. No one was aware of this information, although he could be sure the Gestapo knew and that's why they were watching him closely. Jacque contacted his wireless operator who sent an urgent message to London for advice. Jacque thought they would probably take him out of the country as soon as could be arranged but he hoped not. If he could hide away in another area for a while it might work. He just didn't want to give in and leave even though that was the safest for him.

Jacque was passing information on to Jean Paul whom he trusted with his whole being. He wanted Jean Paul to work with the convent on moving the Jews on to the next stage. It would have to be done a few people at a time and see what happened. Hopefully the Germans wouldn't even realise what was happening. Jacques himself would not be there. He was being airlifted out of France that very night. It was felt too dangerous for him to remain. Either his cover had been blown or they were suspicious and thought he was in communication with the convent.

It was growing dark and Jacque was preparing to leave. Jean Paul wanted to go with him as would be normal to help guide the plane but Jacques wouldn't agree. He didn't want anyone else involved as he didn't know just how closely he was being watched.

He left without telling anyone except Jean Paul. That way there was less chance of anyone informing the Gestapo of his movements. He needed to get away and back to London to pass on everything he knew about the current state of affairs. Sadly he would have to say the convent would be closed to Jews trying to escape the country and being hidden in the convent until everything could be arranged. The convent was no longer a place of safety.

It was completely dark as Jacque waited for the plane to arrive. His hearing very acute, he was on high alert, listening to see if he had been followed and straining for the sound of engines indicating the plane was approaching. He kept low behind some bushes waiting. His ears picked up, he could hear something fast approaching. Vehicles, could it be the plane or lorries indicating the Germans were nearby. He wasn't sure but hoped it was the plane. Was that voices he could hear from some way off? Where was the plane? He needed to get away fast. There was no way he would make it back to Jean Paul alive if he had to turn back. He could only hope the plane would arrive before the Germans found him, for he was sure now that it was the Germans. Had someone tipped them off? Was it just coincidence, but he didn't believe that for one minute.

There was a flash of light. Jacque held his breath then realised a plane was arriving close by now with all lights turned off. The Germans were getting closer. It was a race against time. Who would make it first? He was prepared to make a run for it to the plane when it got close enough. It was fast approaching but there was a sound of gun fire. The Germans had heard the approaching plane as well. This was going to be tricky and the possibility of getting out of there alive was becoming very slim indeed. He knew the time had come. He needed to make a run for it. Hoping to get on the plane alive. He went sprinting as fast as possible towards the plane which was getting closer all the time. He just about had time to climb in than it was lifting into the air again. He was safe but felt sad for he would never see that area of France again. If he was sent back it would be under another name and to a different part of the country possibly disguised with a completely new look. The Gestapo were ruthless and had long memories. They would have him on their records and a photo of him as well.

Chapter Thirteen

Jean Paul drew closer to the convent wondering if he was doing the right thing. He had decided that he should approach Marie in person and introduce himself. It was probable that if he should phone she would be wary about who he was. He needed to explain that Jacques had gone and they needed to discuss the plans he was drawing up to remove the Jews in small groups over the next few weeks.

He hoped it would be just the one contact before things happened. Although the resistance were watching the convent still he felt the less presence the better it would be. He had talked it over with Jacque before he left and it had been agreed on. Jacque would report this back to London if he were to make it safely back.

The bell rang out. The nuns looked at each other, a look of fear on their faces. Was it the Germans again? They hadn't been disturbed by them for a couple of weeks now so had been starting to relax again. Monique stood up and went to the spy hole in the door. She could see a man but he wasn't in German uniform and as far as she could tell there weren't any others standing behind waiting to push their way in.

"Who is it?" she called.

"My name is Jean Paul and I'm here to see the Reverend Mother."

"Who are you?" she asked cautiously.

"The resistance. I'm here in place of Jacques."

Monique carefully opened the door. She knew the name from when Marie had mentioned it to her. She realised this could be a trap and the Germans were just waiting to follow but she had to take a risk and trust him.

"Close the door quickly. I don't think I was seen but you never can tell with the Germans. Can I see the Reverend Mother?"

Monique nodded and led the way still looking behind her as if the Germans were going to jump out at her any minute. They had all become very jumpy over the slightest thing. She knew they should be trusting God to keep them safe but it was very difficult.

She opened the door and curtsied when Marie bade them enter. Marie looked up startled when she saw Jean Paul. He paled when he saw her. He had no idea it was her when he had decided to come in person instead of phoning. Monique didn't say anything although curiosity was getting the better of her. It was clear they knew each other.

"Clara," he murmured.

"It's Marie now," said Marie.

Monique picked up a cold note in her superior's voice and saw a look appear on Marie's face which she had never seen before and couldn't describe it if she had been asked. It made her want to escape from the room. There was obviously ancient history between the two.

At a nod from Marie, Monique quickly made her escape. She went back to the others who were enjoying recreation but she didn't join in the chatter. She remained quiet even when questioned by the others. What was going on in Marie's room? How did they know each other?. There was clearly some animosity between them, on Marie's side anyway. Jean Paul had just been surprised when he saw who it was.

…………..

"What do you want?" asked Marie. "I thought I had made myself clear that you were not to contact me again. Why now after all these years?"

"I was… I mean I didn't know it was you. The last I knew your name was Clara and you lived in Paris with your parents."

"I did but as you can see I'm here now. I'm the Reverend Mother and I would prefer it if you didn't spread my past around. I have a reputation to keep up."

Jean Paul nodded. "I thought you left me for another man. That's what you led me to believe anyway."

"Me leave you? I don't remember it like that. You had an affair with my best friend."

"That was nothing. I told you that. She flirted with me, but it was always you in my mind. There hasn't been anyone else but you in my life since then, but I see you've moved on."

Marie nodded, "I turned to the church unable to face any man. I'd been brought up a Catholic anyway so it just seemed the next logical step really."

"So you ran away," Jean Paul pointed out.

"It wasn't like that. It was another year before they would accept me as a postulant. Like you they were concerned I was escaping you and that wasn't the right attitude for a nun. I was sure this was the right way forward for me and I haven't once regretted it. My parents disowned me when I went into the church. Although Catholics they didn't want this for their children. They felt I was too religious for them."

"I'm sorry."

"Don't be. I am more than fulfilled in the life I have now. I know this was my vocation, I just needed to see it. So yeah, maybe I should be grateful to you for treating me like that. My life could have been very different."

"You could have been just as fulfilled as a wife and mother."

Marie shook her head. "I am the bride of Christ and mother to all who come in here. I have all that I need. Now that's enough of us, that's ancient history. Tell me why you are here and what it has to do with Jacque."

Jean Paul repeated the story, leaving nothing out.

"I didn't realise Jacque was sent from England."

"No one did except me."

"So what is your plan to move the Jews? Where are they going because I will only let them go if I think they're going somewhere safe."

"They are going to another town, of which I am keeping to myself. The less people who know the safer for everyone."

Marie nodded in understanding.

"Other than that I am not prepared to say, but they will be got out of the country to safety. Of course we will not use you to hide anymore Jews as it has become very unsafe for all concerned."

"Ok when will this take place?"

"Tonight after dark the first group of four will go in pairs chatting away so they'll just appear to be good friends. Also leaving in pairs is less likely to attract attention to them."

"I'll be in touch when the next lot are to go. First I need to make sure the plan is successful before getting anyone else out. Oh and you are to tell no one. That way we can be sure the Germans don't find out anything before it happens."

"The nuns will be curious, I have to tell them something."

"I'm sure you can come up with an answer. You used to be full of answers to everything when I last knew you and I'm sure you haven't changed much since then really. Now I bid you goodbye," this last was said with a hint of coldness in his voice.

"Ok I will follow your orders. I only want the best for the Jews. Stay safe Jean Paul," she said, her voice softening a little for the first time since he had entered.

He nodded but said nothing, turning to leave the room. He didn't want her to see the tears in his eyes. Seeing her again was stirring up so many memories from the past that he had put away, or so he'd thought. He had never got over losing her and wished he'd never been turned by her best friend.

Marie sat staring into space thinking about the past. Not once had she regretted what happened. The church was where she belonged. In some ways Caterina, her friend, had done her a good turn. It had shown her the way forward for her life which was right for her. She had been happy with Jean Paul until she found out he'd cheated on her. He had been good to her treating her like a princess, spoiling her with many presents. She had thought they would get married one day and live happily ever after just like the princesses in fairy stories. It wasn't to be though. It seemed he had been turned by a bit of flirting. Marie had lost her boyfriend and her best friend in one day. Totally bereft she had fallen into depression, refusing to leave her room, failing to respond to her parents entreaties.

One day she had felt moved to go to a church. She got up and went out without telling her parents where she was going. Sat in the church quietly she had felt something stir within her, a feeling that stayed with her long after she left. She repeated this, in fact it became a ritual. Thoughts started racing around in her mind that she should do more than go to church but she should make church her life.

Her parents had reacted in horror when she finally told them of her plans. They hoped it was a reaction to losing Jean

Paul and tried to point out this, but Marie was not to be swayed. It was the church for her and that was definite. Her parents went as far as saying they would disown her if she went into the church. Nothing would persuade Marie otherwise, so she entered the church, lost her parents and hadn't looked back since.

Marie shook her head to bring herself out of her reverie. Jean Paul had really stirred things up for her, making her think of the past. It hadn't distressed her, that walk down memory lane. She remained happy with her choice.

Chapter Fourteen

Marie went down to see the Jews to discuss with them the latest plans. She was glad that something had finally been put in place as they had been hiding out in dim light for too long now. They were starting to get restless and thinking they would have been better off being taken by the Germans and disappearing to God knows where.

"Ok now you know what's happening I need you to decide who will be in the first four to leave tonight."

Marie looked around at them and saw relief on some of their faces. Yes, this was the right time. They would go mad if left much longer in this confined space with no actual daylight.

"Please take me," said a small voice at the back. "I can't stand enclosed spaces."

Marie looked across at the older lady and smiled. "That's fine Mrs Goldberg."

The other three were decided by who drew the shortest straw. The four who were to leave were smiling for the first time in a long time, letting Marie know she was doing the right thing. How she hoped it would work out.

Marie was to wait until she got the signal then they were to leave in pairs. The second couple were to leave fifteen minutes after the first if everything went according to plan.

Marie sat anxiously in her office waiting for the time to come. The signal would be given and she would rush down and let them out through the underground passage. Going out that way would take them up into the hills behind the convent. So far as the resistance were concerned there were no Germans watching that way so they must have no knowledge of this which was a relief to everyone.

…………

It was starting to get dark. Marie waited anxiously for the call. When the phone rung she jumped as if startled. It shouldn't have done as she knew it was to happen. She didn't answer and waited for it to stop before ringing again and repeated this one last time. It had been decided to do it like this in case the Germans should learn of the plan and try to flush the Jews out.

Breathing a sigh of relief, Marie went and let the first pair out. She gave a smile and bade them good luck. She blessed them and the two Jews left. They were to be met at the entrance to the tunnel and instructions would then be given to them. If all went well she would receive the same signal for the second pair. She couldn't stay with the Jews for long needing to get back to intercept the code again in a short while.

Marie waited, and waited a bit longer. Starting to get nervous she glanced at her watch. It was half an hour since the first pair had left. Something must have gone wrong, she was sure of it. It had been decided that if anything went wrong Jean Paul would not phone until the next day so she would know the difference between the code and a phone call to tell her of a problem.

Forty five minutes later the phone rang. Marie relaxed slightly, although still anxious. She rushed to the Jews to repeat the process of releasing the other two who were to leave that night. She found pandemonium when she got down there. Some were arguing, worrying over her lack of appearance, sure that something had gone wrong.

"Ok listen up," called Marie into the noise. "It's time for the second pair to say goodbye and move on."

Silence fell, and the pair so churned up inside actually refused to go. They had been so caught up in worry that it had failed they couldn't bring themselves to leave in case they fell into the hands of the Germans.

"It's all right," said Marie, realising what was happening. "It's safe. The code could not have reached the ears of the Germans and I received it a few minutes ago. I don't know why it is later than planned. It could be the first two took longer to get out than at first thought."

The two shook their heads still not sure they wanted to go. They preferred to wait in the basement area where they were at least semi safe. Marie couldn't persuade them. All she could do was go back and wait for Jean Paul to ring the following day. She was sure he wouldn't be pleased as one thing she knew about him was that he expected everyone to fall in with his plans. She was sure he couldn't have changed that much over the years. In fact, thinking about it now Marie realised she'd had a lucky escape. This facet about him probably would have made him a control freak and one thing she hated was being controlled.

Chapter Fifteen

Marie answered the phone with much trepidation. She was sure it was Jean Paul and she didn't want to be the one to explain what had happened.

"What happened?" he asked, before she had a chance to say anything. There was no hello just those two words. He was not happy just as she'd surmised.

"The second pair were reluctant to go because the code came so much later than we expected."

"It took longer than we hoped to for the first pair to emerge. I put the code through as soon as they did. As far as I know they reached the other safe house without any problem or none that I've heard as yet."

"What do we do now?" asked Marie.

"Well I need to consider if it's worth the safety of my network to remove more of the Jews if they are going to be difficult."

"They're not being difficult, they are very scared which anyone would be in their situation."

"I get that, but I'm trying to help them and they are throwing it back in my face."

"That isn't it at all. They are just frightened as I already said. Put yourself in their situation and maybe you would understand how they're feeling."

Jean Paul went quiet before saying, "I feel as if you're putting obstacles in the way. Maybe you like the feeling of danger there is while the Jews are with you."

"It's not that, and I'm quite insulted that you would think that of me."

"You've changed Clara."

"Not really," said Marie. "And don't call me Clara, you know my name is Marie now."

"You'll always be Clara to me."

Marie shook her head, knowing he wouldn't see it over the phone.

"Anyway we have to sort out the way forward now Jean Paul."

"I suppose I'll have to let the next lot out. I'd been planning on next week but maybe the pair from yesterday would prefer to go sooner since they bottled it."

"What slang you're using. You used to speak such perfect French."

"I guess I've changed as well. It's been a long time."

"I know, and if we are to work together we have to try and get along. We need to trust each other."

"That's a hard one. You just disappeared from my life without a word. You didn't respond to any of my letters. I called round to see you and your parents wouldn't let me in on your instructions."

"What was I supposed to do. I caught you with my best friend. Don't you think it's hard for me as well to trust you now."

"I suppose so," admitted Jean Paul grudgingly.

"Well we need to forget this and think of the Jews right now and what's best for them."

"My instinct's telling me to leave it a week and then try again. It's up to you who goes. This time though I've learned a lesson and I'll leave it longer in between each pair leaving."

"Sounds a good plan," said Marie.

The phone went dead. She supposed it was a bit of an awkward situation for both of them. But he could at least have said bye.

She sighed as she stood up preparing to go and let the Jews know what was happening. She hadn't told any of the nuns, not even Monique, that two had gone and more were to go.

She stretched and gave a yawn, tired and stiff from sitting so still. She hadn't been able to sleep worried about the situation and unable to stop thinking about her past life with Jean Paul and wondering how different her life could have been if they had stayed together as she had planned in her mind. It was a pity Jean Paul had strayed.

"Ok listen up everyone," Marie said when she got down to the basement. "There are to be more going next week as it's felt too close if more leave sooner. Decide who amongst you are to go next."

"What about the children? I can't go without my two little ones," said Francine.

"I've not heard about any plans to move the children as yet. I will ask next time I have contact. I do understand what you are saying and accept that you don't want to be separated from your children. It is only right."

It didn't take long to decide who were the next four to go. Many of them were in family units with children so were saying no unless they went together. Marie kept it in her mind to ask about this when she next had word from Jean Paul.

....

"Well?" asked Jean Paul at the start of the conversation. "Has it been sorted who the next ones are to leave."

"Yes," said Marie, "But we have a problem. What about the children as many are refusing to leave unless their children are with them."

"That's ok as long as the children are kept quiet and behave themselves. I don't want noise and attention drawn to them. Even more important as they are leaving after curfew so would be in extra trouble if caught."

"Great, I'll tell them. I'll suggest only those with older children go for the moment for safety reasons."

....

Marie relayed the conversation causing many sighs of relief amongst the Jews. They were mostly family units who didn't want to be split up. They were going to leave it as had already been decided for next time and after that try and move families and see what happened.

Marie wondered whether she should tell anyone what was happening concerning the Jews. She was inclined to at least tell Monique but didn't want to risk being overheard if she decided to keep the rest in the dark. There hadn't been any further raids since Julianne had been killed so it looked like she was the traitor despite her protestations of innocence. In fact the German presence was lessening so maybe they'd given up, at least for the moment.

Deciding to keep it to herself she went back to her room, rubbing her tired eyes. How she wished she could close them and drift off to sleep. She went to the chapel first as she realised she had only a short time before Matins began. She might benefit from the peace and quiet that could be felt there.

Kneeling at the altar she bowed her head and prayed to Our Lady to intercede with the most high God. She prayed the Jews would successfully get away and remain safe and hidden until they could be got out of the country. It would be difficult where the children were concerned as it would be a lot of climbing in the mountains to get over the border into a safe country.

She turned, hearing a noise behind her. It was the arrival of the rest of the community. She didn't feel ready to lead but knew she had to keep things as normal as possible for their own sakes.

It was Monique that noticed Marie was a little distracted and wondered why. It was unusual. She was usually very with it and ready to lead but not this morning. She didn't seem even slightly prepared for the day ahead. She tried to concentrate on Marie's halted, familiar words but found it difficult. There was nothing she could do until she could catch her afterwards and get the truth out of her. She was surprised Marie hadn't already spoken to her as she usually heard what was going on before anyone else. She felt a little hurt but knew Marie would have a good reason not to say anything.

"Marie, can I have a word please?" asked Monique, catching up with her on the way out of the chapel.

"I'm not sure that's a good idea," said Marie, still distracted.

"Mother it's me," said Monique.

"You don't want to know and anyway I don't want to potentially put you in danger."

"Is this something to do with the Jews then?"

"I can't tell you," repeated Marie and left it at that as she didn't want anyone else finding out about the Jews.

"It is isn't it? You're not saying because you don't want anyone overhearing and reporting us. We've had our fair share of problems with the Gestapo lately."

Marie nodded but stayed silent. The others had slipped away by this time but she felt as if the walls might have ears and report her.

"Why don't we stay here and you tell me. We know there's no one else around at the moment. Everyone's gone about their business for the day. We won't be disturbed."

Marie nodded, but still said nothing.

Monique led the way to the altar where they could have a whispered conversation which couldn't be over heard. Monique was all to aware of the danger if they were to be informed upon by one of the nuns. No one could be trusted. Recent experience showed that.

"Right then, now we can have a chat about what's on your mind."

Marie shook her head.

"Come on," said Monique. "You should share it or the others are going to notice you're not your usual self. It's obvious you are distracted by something and it doesn't take much to guess it's connected with the Jews."

"Jacque has gone. He won't be back. I've been in contact with Jean Paul." Marie blushed as she mentioned his name. As her cheeks felt flaming she cursed her ability to blush so easily which gave things away, especially to someone like Monique who knew her so well.

"You know Jean Paul?"

Marie nodded. She knew she could trust Monique not to spread the information round the others but was still reluctant to share anything about her past life with anyone.

"We were seeing each other. I thought we'd get married and live happily ever after. It didn't work out like that," said Marie, with a trace of bitterness in her words.

"What happened?" asked the gentle voice of Monique.

"He had an affair with my best friend and I found out about it. We split up. I was heartbroken at the time but am glad as I have a much better life now, here serving God. He was able to reach me in my despair and I responded to His call on my life."

"But it still affects you."

"It didn't. I never think about it, that is until Jean Paul came back into my life and now I can't get out of my mind what happened."

"You must forgive. Ask our Lady to help you."

Marie said, "I'm trying."

"Now we've got that out of the way you can tell me what he's said as I can't believe all you talk about is your history together."

"A couple of Jews left us. More will be going next week. They are going in pairs as it's less likely to draw attention to them. If that's successful we are going to have a go at getting family groups out."

"Wow, I'm so glad it's working. We really need to get rid of them for everyone's sake."

"I don't know anything more. Jean Paul felt it best if it was on a need to know basis only."

"That makes sense," said Monique. "Thank you for telling me. I'll go now before anyone misses me."

Marie sighed as she was alone once again. She looked up at the cross before her and bowed before she too stood up and left. She loved leading the convent but there were times when it seemed like too much of a responsibility. She was a strong, merciful leader, much loved by those around her. They knew they could go to her at anytime and she would be there for them.

Those who sinned found only compassion met them, understood by their Reverend Mother and found forgiveness.

Marie sat in her room, staring into space as was her wont these days. Oh how she prayed the war would be over and the Germans gone from France. There was no sign of that happening, at least as far as the news was concerned. She did realise what they heard was what the Germans wanted them to know. It was just propaganda.

As she sat there in a world of her own she began thinking of Eve. What was she to do. If it was her alone she would be protected under her guise as a nun, but it wasn't that simple. She had a child who was hidden away with the other Jews. Eve slipped down there everyday to see her daughter and spend as much time as she could with her. Marie thought they would have to leave at some point as it wouldn't be right to split the pair up and send Francesca away, not understanding why she wasn't with her mummy.

That would be a conversation next time she spoke to Jean Paul. She could reconcile herself to Jean Paul being back in her life as long as they didn't meet. There was no reason why they should, in fact it was better if they didn't because it would probably be even more painful for both of them.

There was a tentative knock on the door and Bernadette entered. "Sorry to disturb you but there is a German at the door."

Marie looked up, alarmed at such news.

"There is only one of them," said Bernadette, at which Marie visibly relaxed.

"Ok bring him here. I should see him on my own territory."

Hans Biedecker introduced himself as he entered and bowed to Marie.

"I have great respect for your church," he said.

"You are a Catholic?"

"Yes. I have always been to church until now. It is my interest in the church that brought me here today. As you know we have been taking great interest in you because of information that you are sheltering Jews. All our searches have shown nothing so we assume it was malicious gossip by someone. My commanding officer and the Gestapo are not convinced and may raid at any time. I am coming to warn you that you are now very much on our radar. You could be interned. No one knows I am here but I felt it was my duty as a Catholic to warn you in advance. If you have Jews here I advise you let them go as soon as can be arranged just in case you are interned in one of our camps."

"I thank you for your warning and advice Herr Biedecker. I will think on it and decide what I need to do."

Hans bowed low again and left. Marie sat in silence before sending for Monique. She needed to discuss the situation before speaking to Jean Paul.

Monique looked startled at the sight of Marie. She had a troubled look on her face and solemnity around her mouth and eyes replacing the gentle love which was always there.

"I've just had a visit from a German wanting to warn me that we could be interned at anytime so should get rid of the Jews as soon as possible."

"So they still believe we're hiding them."

"I'm not sure but he must suspect it. He appeared to be on our side but of course he could be pretending to see if he could get more information out of me."

"Have you spoken to Jean Paul?"

"Not yet. I wanted to hear from you first. My mind is all over the place. I don't know what to do for the best."

"Well, it could be a trick to try and flush out the Jews. If it's genuine of course then we must take it seriously."

"It didn't occur to me it could be lies. I took it as a real threat to us. I need to speak to the resistance and see what the suggest. If they know this German they might have some idea of the truth behind his warning."

Monique nodded.

"Thanks for that. It helped me work through what I need to do. Can you send Eve to me as she needs to decide what she wants to do for herself and her daughter. She could stick with us and take her chances that her Jewish status never gets discovered or she leaves with her daughter and takes her chances in the open."

Chapter Sixteen

"I have heard that as well from my contacts," said Jean Paul, speaking to Marie about the situation.

"What should we do? I have spoken to Eve our Jew who is living as a nun and she has decided she wants to leave with her daughter. I agree with her as it might be safer. She doesn't want to be away from Francesca for very long. She's already lost her husband she can't lose her daughter as well."

"I understand that. It's up to you when you arrange for them to leave. My suggestion is that we increase the number of times the Jews leave in a week. I don't think anything will happen immediately from what you say. He was giving you time. We must trust him that he does want what's best for you. There are a few good Germans out there who hate what is happening in the world as much as we do."

"The one problem I have is that the rest of the nuns will notice if Eve isn't amongst us anymore. The whole idea was that no one else knew what was happening to avoid anymore informants."

"I see your problem. Maybe leave her until towards the end if she is happy to wait that long."

Marie agreed and the phone call ended. She sat there for a moment lost in thought. It was the bell for chapel that brought her back. She stood up and with a heavy heart went about her day as if everything were normal.

. . . .

"Eve can you wait a second please, I need to speak to you in private."

Eve looked startled. She immediately cast around in her mind for some accidental sin she had committed. Although she wasn't officially a nun she was observing the same rules as the real nuns did to make it authentic to anyone watching.

"Don't worry, you're not in trouble. You've settled to this life surprisingly well."

"I've had to. I've just watched the others and copied them. I'm a quick learner."

"I've seen that. No, what I want to speak to you about is when you and Francesca might leave. I've spoken to my contact and he suggests you should be one of the last to leave so as to keep up the pretence before the other nuns."

"But they know I'm not really a nun," pointed out Eve, none to happy at the idea that she should be one of the last to leave. It seemed to her it might be too late.

"Yes, but they don't know that the Jews are slowly leaving us. We can't risk them knowing in case someone decides to inform on us."

"I thought that was sorted now and the informant had been dealt with."

"She was but the less people who know what we're doing the better," Marie paused before continuing, "I take it you're not happy to wait?"

Eve shook her head. "It seems frightening. If we wait it might be too late and I owe it to Francesca to get out while we can. I want her to survive at all costs. She is an innocent in this broken world. If it were just me I wouldn't mind so much."

Marie looked sober. Put like that she understood where Eve was coming from. It was a very difficult situation and hard to know what to do for the best. "Ok," said Marie at last. "I'll think about it and report back to the resistance and see what they say." Marie paused before continuing, "Thank you for listening and understanding. I realise how trapped you must feel, trying to be one of us whilst being set apart. I'll do all I can to protect you and Francesca but if the Germans take us all I can't guarantee what will happen then. They could shoot us all or send us to their camps that I've heard so much about and if my sources are to be believed they are not nice places. No one ever returns and many die or are killed. Starvation is rife. I definitely don't want that for you and Francesca. I think you'd be split up once there and I can't allow that to happen. You have to get away if the two of you are to have any sort of life."

Eve nodded, "Thank you. I know you'll do your best."

………

It was later that day when Monique knocked on the door. "Is everything all right? I've been knocking and you haven't answered. It's not like you."

"Sorry a bit distracted. Eve longs to leave here but doesn't want to wait until the end in case we are taken before then. She's mostly thinking of Francesca."

"She's such a sweetheart. I can understand where Eve is coming from. She's putting her daughter first which of course she must."

"I know you're right but it does complicate things somewhat. No one is supposed to know what we are doing and now they'll work it out quickly. The more people who know the more chance there is for the Germans to find out."

The phone rang. Monique quickly dropped her curtsey and went to leave the room. Marie indicated she wanted her to stay but Monique shook her head and left.

"Hello."

"Hello," said a voice on the other end. "Be ready to move in two weeks."

"What," shrieked Marie. "I can't have all the Jews moved and see to us at the same time."

"That's the message I have from my source at their headquarters. They want you all under arrest immediately but a voice has spoken up for you and it has been agreed to take you all then. Don't forget I warned you of this before the Germans even intruded on us."

"I know. It was inevitable really. I'll speed up the Jews evacuation."

"Great," said Jean Paul.

Marie was glad when the day ended. It had been difficult organising the Jews and at the same time waiting for the door to be crashed in. She assumed when the Germans went for them they would just get in without knocking politely and waiting. That wasn't their style.

Eve was going to have to go sooner than expected which was a shame. She had fitted in so well they kept forgetting she wasn't a nun under their jurisdiction. It would be hard to say good bye to her and Francesca. If it hadn't been for the child then Eve could have stayed with them but the Germans would get suspicious if a child was revealed in their midst. They were already highly alert expecting anything that the best way was right under their noses. They didn't look so close to home usually.

Chapter Seventeen

"I don't know if the easiest way would be to ask our friendly German to help us," said Jean Paul.

"Is that a good idea. He could be pretending to be nice to get us to trust him and then hope we'll slip up."

"I'd thought of that. Do give me some credit. I'm not that stupid. Jacque wouldn't have left me in charge if he thought I was. I'm an intelligent guy as you should know. I never struck you as dumb did I?"

"Er no," said Marie, sounding suitably chastened. "If you feel it's right then speak to him and let me know. I accept you are more aware of them and their views than I am shut away from the world."

"Not for much longer I'm afraid. I'll try and get some idea of where they will take you. It's possible Gestapo headquarters as they still think you are guilty of hiding Jews on the premises."

"They won't find any the same as they never have done when they have searched."

"I know that but they do tend to believe the informants. It doesn't occur to them that people tell them things out of pure malice sometimes just because they like causing trouble or don't like the person they are informing on."

The phone call finished and Marie sat there thinking. She didn't know when she should tell the others what was happening so they would be prepared for it or if she should even tell them at all. Certainly the Jews needed to be gone and fast, including Eve and her daughter. Why did the world have to be so complicated? Why couldn't they remain innocent shut away from the world? The Germans were no respecter of anyone or any organisation including religion.

Chapter Eighteen

It was time for Eve and Francesca to leave. They were going together with another mother and child who were on their own.

Francesca was treating it like a game, too young to know the danger they were putting themselves in. Eve was relieved that she remained a child and wanted that to continue to be the case, but who knew what awaited them on the outside where they would be more vulnerable. Steps were taken to ensure their safety but was anyone safe these days?

It had been impossible to hide from the other nuns that Eve was leaving but they were only told minutes beforehand to avoid any temptation to tell the Germans what was going on and when. If anyone did they should be long gone before any search could take place.

Many of the nuns on hearing the news became teary eyed. They had become fond of Eve during the time she had been with them.

....

They were hurrying along the passage way that would take them back into the outside world. They knew there would be someone at the other end who would give them instructions of what to do next. They went in silence in case they could be overheard by anyone who shouldn't be there. It was hard to keep the two children quiet as they were excited and wanted to know where they were going. They thought it was just a grown up version of hide and seek.

"Shh," whispered Eve as Francesca tried to speak in a loud voice. "You have to be quiet, remember what we said."

Francesca nodded and Eve put her arm around her daughter and pulled her close. They were nearing the exit of the tunnel and talking was strictly forbidden now. They could have no idea of the danger that was awaiting them.

They slowly made their way out, the two mums going first to make sure it was safe. Even now, when in such danger, they put their daughters wellbeing and safety first. Any trouble and the children had been told to run back the way they had come. They were given an agreed code so they would be let back in at the other end. No one knew this except for Marie and the two children. That way the Germans wouldn't find the way in if they tried going down that route.

"Shh," said a voice as they came out into the open.

Eve looked around her. It had seemed like forever that they had been out in the fresh air enjoying life. Unfortunately that time was long gone and who knew when or if it would ever come back. They lived in very uncertain times and no one could ever know what was going to come.

They stopped at hearing the voice and waited.

"I'm Charles, and I'm going to take you to the train station. I already have your tickets and travel passes that you need. I'm glad to see none of you are wearing your yellow star. That should help. You must remember you are Catholics if approached and asked, although it is unlikely you will need that information. The more you know the better you will stay out of harms way."

The group nodded, not speaking.

"Ok we need to get off quickly. We are going along there," he said pointing to the right. "Keep low behind the bushes. It may be uncomfortable to stay bent low but is very necessary until we reach the road."

The group made their way as fast as possible. Not only were they breaking curfew but they looked highly suspicious creeping along the bushes.

"Quick, down," said Charles, catching the sound of lorries drawing up.

Something was definitely happening and he didn't know what. Until he knew they weren't going anywhere. He didn't like it. The sound grew closer. He didn't know whether they should make a run for it and hope for the best or stay put. Both could get them into great trouble or help keep them safe. He opted for the stay. If the Germans did in fact see them run they would probably open fire and they would all be dead. That wasn't part of the plan.

"Ok," said Charles, having come to a decision. "It may be best to turn back"

The two mothers however, were rooted to the spot, too frightened to move. The fear was being transferred to the two girls who began whimpering. The women put their hands over the girls mouths to try and keep them quiet and hoping the danger would pass.

The sounds of lorries stopped nearby, too close for Charles. He didn't like it. Something had gone very wrong with their plans. The others had all got away no problem.

"Come on," said Charles impatiently. "We can't risk staying here, we'll be caught. We need to go back the way we came. Fortunately we haven't got far."

Eve began to hurry as fast as she could but she was the only one.

Charles changed his mind and said, "We'll continue going forward if you can't go back. But staying here is not an option. We're sure to be caught and I can assure you the consequences won't be pleasant. You should know that as Jews having to remain in hiding for so long."

"STOP!!" called a voice from the side. "Who are you and what are you doing out at this time. The curfew."

Charles spoke, "We know but one of our daughters is very sick and we need to get to the hospital."

"What's wrong with her," asked the German, highly suspicious.

"We don't know, she developed a rash and her face has swollen and she has vomited."

Charles felt this a safe story as Eve was by now out of sight leaving him with the other mother and the two children.

Eve looked behind her expecting to see Francesca. Realising her daughter hadn't followed her she turned back. Hearing the

German voice she knew that wasn't an option she had to keep going and hope her daughter would be all right. She had no choice but to trust Charles. To be split up from her daughter, not knowing if she would ever see her again was heartbreaking. It was almost too much to bear. No choice remained but to get back into the convent and relative safety for the moment.

………

"Where's Francesca and the other two," said Marie when she saw the tear stained face of Eve.

"The Germans turned up. I was the only one who turned back. The Germans now have them."

Marie took Eve into her arms and held her. She knew how difficult this was for Eve. First losing her husband and now her small daughter. When would this all end?

Marie was speaking to Jean Paul later that night. He was telling her what had happened after Eve left. "Our people saw the Germans approach the group. We don't know what Charles said to them but it didn't help as they were herded on to the back of the lorry and driven off to the headquarters. My worry is not for Charles but for the children. That they will tell the truth if asked questions which they surely will be."

"What can we do about Eve?"

"You'll have to keep her I'm afraid. She was well disguised as one of you lot so she'll be safe enough for the moment anyway."

Marie nodded then realised Jean Paul couldn't see her nod over the phone. It was true though, Eve was safe although distraught as any mother would be. "How did they know there would be anyone out in that area at this time?"

"I'm not sure although I think someone must have spoken to them."

"Another traitor?" queried Marie.

"Unfortunately I think so. Otherwise it could be the same traitor as before if we got the wrong person."

"Oh no, I hope not," said Marie. "Although she did protest her innocence."

"Fortunately all the Jews have now gone except for Eve and she should be safe enough under your protection. I just hope you can stay safely there for as long as possible, but I have my doubts."

Eve looked up with a small sad smile on her face when Marie approached. "Just to let you know the others were herded on to those awful lorries and taken away. I am so sorry."

Marie waited for the outpouring of tears that she thoroughly expected but Eve had done all the crying and had no more left.

"You are to remain with us as a nun which I'm pleased to say. That should keep you safe enough for now, until they come for us as they surely will. At least you won't be treated as a Jew when they do arrive so should be more respected."

"Do the Germans respect anyone?" asked Monique, overhearing the last part of Marie's speech.

"Very true, and while they suspect us of helping Jews it will be even worse. Hopefully they'll just take us elsewhere where no one knows of our alleged Jews and we'll be treated better."

"They only treat their own Nazis better. If you're not a fully paid up member of the Party then you're in trouble," said Monique, a bitterness creeping into her voice.

"Nevertheless we are called to forgive our enemies so that we must do."

"I know but I don't think I can. We've lost two of our own to them already and that's not including Julieanne."

"You need to pray for the ability to forgive," said Marie. She knew she was sounding more stern than she should as she too, struggled with this issue. She couldn't let the others know though. She was supposed to be an example to them but she was only human herself with the same faults and failings. If only the priest were still coming they could get proper guidance and maybe a way to forgive.

They really were missing confession and the partaking of the blessed sacrament the body and blood of Jesus. She wished the priest hadn't been such a coward and given in to the Germans and put himself first. Although who knew how they would behave in the same circumstances. It wasn't as easy for him out in the real world, having to live alongside their enemy.

Chapter Nineteen

"What's wrong?" asked Monique, coming upon Eve and finding her head in her hands weeping inconsolably.

Eve was unable to answer, being completely beyond words. Monique sat beside her putting an arm on her shoulder and waited quietly. Just letting Eve know she wasn't alone and someone cared. Monique wanted to go for Marie but felt it wasn't wise to leave Eve while she was like this.

Eve had seemed so strong, meeting every crisis that occurred but now it had all become too much. Maybe they should have been more aware of this, thought Monique now. It can't be easy trying to disguise yourself as being from a completely different religion and having a daughter who needed to be hidden and now no one knew what had happened after their capture. Personally Monique had her doubts over Francesca's survival. Not only was she a Jew but so very young and unlikely to be of use to the Germans and therefore expendable. The camps they heard about were terrible places according to Marie's contact in the resistance movement in their area. No way was she going to voice these thoughts to Eve or to anyone else though. It was of paramount importance that Eve was given some hope that one day she would see her daughter again. No one could continue without hope, it was vital to their very survival especially in the days they were living through and enduring.

Eve continued to sob, too far gone to realise there was someone beside her wanting to offer comfort. Her heart was breaking in two. She was alone, her family gone and she didn't know if she could carry on. Maybe she should walk out and give herself up to the Germans and let them do their worst. Anything was better than what she was going through now. The agony, the pain it was all too much. She had kept it inside for so long, needing to be strong for her daughter but now she had disappeared, captured by the Germans.

"I'm just going to get Marie," whispered Monique. "She should be able to help more than I can. I'll be back in a minute."

Monique was true to her word and was back very quickly with Marie in tow. Marie took one look at the other woman and put her arm around her, suggesting Monique go the other side and between them they helped get Eve to Marie's room. Monique got up to leave after sitting Eve down in a comfortable chair. Marie shook her head and motioned for her to stay. Eve could do with as much as support as possible.

Eve's sobs showed no sign of abating. The two nuns waited in silence just holding Eve between them.

Marie was getting worried, this was getting out of hand and there seemed no let up in sight. If only they had access to a medical professional but that was impossible now as well. Their very life as a community of nuns was being stifled, leaving them more isolated than they should be. They were stuck with no solution except wait for the inevitable to happen.

As nuns they already lived an austere life and would be somewhat equipped to deal with being incarcerated by the Germans. Eve however, was a different matter. She wasn't a nun but was being forced to take up the religion just to stay safe.

"Come on Eve," said Marie. "Try and stop crying now. We're getting worried about you."

Eve continued to sob her heart out as if she hadn't heard them. Her crying now taking on a hysterical note. All the pent up anguish that had been bottled up for the last few months since her husband was taken and ending up in the convent had to find some outlet.

"What are we to do?" mouthed Monique.

Marie shrugged, also out of her depth here.

The phone rang at that moment startling them all. Eve stopped crying for a moment. Marie took the phone and listened without saying anything other than confirming who she was. She looked across at Eve which told Monique there was some news but due to the set of Marie's mouth it wasn't good news.

Marie put the phone down and gave a slight shake of her head at Monique who sighed, guessing what had happened and wondering how Eve would react when told as she surely must be. It wouldn't be fair to keep it from her and would only make things worse in the long term if she were to find out later and realise they had kept it from her. After all it affected her and she had a right to know.

"Eve, can you listen to me," said Marie quietly sitting back down next to her.

Eve gave a small nod of her head but didn't say anything. She looked quite a sight. Her eyes bloodshot and swollen and face blotchy from all the tears. Her appearance was the least of her worries though.

"That was my contact with the resistance. He told me that Charles has just been shot and the other three were loaded on to the cattle truck ready to be shipped elsewhere, probably to one of the camps he has heard about.

Eve said nothing and Marie wasn't sure if she had heard or understood what had just been said.

"I'm so sorry," said Monique.

Eve still didn't react, she continued sitting there staring into space. Marie felt that things couldn't get much worse for Eve. She had lost her entire family and was on her own except for the nuns and who knew what would happen to them in the near future. Marie chose not to dwell on it.

She was more concerned with what else Jean Paul had said. He had done a bit of digging around and discovered that someone had told the Germans what was to happen and where, which is how they had known where to find them and what time. This meant there was still a traitor amongst them. Maybe they had got it so wrong and Julieanne had been telling the truth about her innocence. Marie couldn't bear the thought of it and had her death on her conscience. She wished she knew who and how it was communicated because the other nuns had only known about it minutes before Eve and Francesca had left. She could have sworn there hadn't been time for anyone to say anything.

The walls of the convent were so high and the nuns couldn't see out beyond their courtyard so couldn't have signalled a message in any way. It was a complete mystery and one that Marie didn't like. Could it really have been Eve as had already been suggested. She had been the only one who knew in advance. Surely not, Marie was so sure Eve was who she said she was, a Jew trying to avoid the Germans and being rounded up. She had lost her husband and now her small daughter was gone.

Marie sighed, it was so very difficult. It was awful living in a small community as they did at the convent and knowing there was someone who couldn't be trusted and no way of finding out who it was.

"That was a big sigh," said Monique, coming to Marie quietly. Monique was light on her feet and often no one knew she was approaching.

"Oh I'm just thinking about Jean Paul and the latest information."

"What's that?" asked Monique.

"Nothing. It's ok. I don't want to burden you with my problems."

"No come on. Tell me. It might help."

"I suppose so." Marie went on to explain to Monique what had happened.

Monique gasped when she heard there was still a traitor amongst them. "Who can it be? We've all been here years. The only person who hasn't is Eve but she seems genuine. She's distraught at losing her husband and child, not knowing if she'll ever see them again."

"I know. I don't think it's Eve. If it isn't that means there is someone here who's doing it. This issue just spreads mistrust amongst us where as before there was mostly peace and harmony in our little community."

"I don't know what to suggest. It has to be someone and we need to find out fast, only make sure we get it right this time."

"That's basically what Jean Paul said."

"I'll listen out and see what I can come up with and then let you know. Don't despair. If we both work on it we should be able to sort this out but I will be glad when it's all over."

Marie nodded. She did feel a sense of relief having shared the burden she had to bear as Reverend Mother of that community. The times they lived in were too hard for the strongest of people. She wished she could understand the motive for informing the Germans then maybe she would be able to work out who it was. It was a blow to realise they had got it so wrong. The obvious person wasn't the one after all. She felt guilty sending the wrong person to their death.

That night Marie tossed and turned wishing she knew what was really going on as well as wondering when the Germans would be coming for them. No one would care as they were aloof and distant from the local population who just saw the high walls of the convent. They were supposed to be a place of safety for the Jews or anyone needing sanctuary but instead they were a place of danger, more so than the outside world at that present time.

Chapter Twenty

"I can try and get you out before the Germans arrive," said Jean Paul when speaking to Marie a few weeks later.

"No, we'll go together. I don't want favouritism. They would know something was wrong if I wasn't here."

"I don't mean just you it's everyone. You still think there is something special about you don't you."

Marie blushed. How could she have thought Jean Paul still wanted the best for her when she had been the one to break off the relationship.

"Anyway, have you any more thoughts on who is the informant?" asked Jean Paul changing the subject.

"None at all. I keep thinking about it. It's going round and round in my head but I still can't come up with anyone. If I think I have the answer I immediately come up with a reason why it can't be that person. It doesn't help that I got it badly wrong last time so I'm afraid of doing that this time without proof."

"I understand your concern. You are in more danger though all the time that person is amongst you."

"I know, but at least things are a bit safer without the Jews here."

"I'm not so sure I agree with you there. We don't really know what the informant is up to or why they've decided to ally themselves with the Germans."

"What exactly are you trying to say?" asked Marie.

"They could be making up things about your activities."

"They must really hate us to do that. I don't see anyone here fitting into that category. All the nuns have been with us for years and we've discounted Eve already."

"I agree it's unlikely to be Eve. She is genuine, I checked her background out thoroughly and it matches all she's told you. It is beyond me to check out all of you nuns because you've all changed your names and renounced the world and your families."

"I don't have access to anyone's past life either and anyway they have all been here years."

"I've just had a thought, is it possible that it's someone who wanted to get the Reverend Mother position when it was given to you? They could be holding a grudge."

"But it's not personal surely they wouldn't want to get the Jews caught."

"It's possible you're right. The way I see it though is that they would be making life more difficult for you which is their main objective. They may even have assumed that you would be taken as well because of your association with the Jews and allowing them to hide out in your convent. It would be something that you had to know about and agree to before it happened."

"And if I were taken it would leave the position free for them to take over in my absence."

"Exactly."

Marie pulled a face. Anyone seeing her would have seen the anguish there. Was there really someone amongst them who detested her so much? In which case they were sinning badly, and not having received absolution at confession.

"You've gone quiet, what are you thinking?"

"Nothing really. My minds a bit of a blank."

"Understandably I've given you a bit of a shock. Can you really not think of anyone who could have stored up such hatred of you."

"No one. Everyone seems at peace and happy here."

"It could be that you're being incredibly naïve. Why don't you let me come and see all of you together. I may be able to see something you've missed because you're to close to the situation."

"I'm not sure that's a good idea. You're male after all and we don't encourage visitors."

"Normally that would hold true, but circumstances are slightly different now. We have been taken over by a brutal enemy, a harsh regime that shows no mercy."

"Ok," said Marie slowly. Very reluctant but unable to see any other solution except to follow what Jean Paul said.

"Great. If it's ok I'll come straight away. If you don't mind I'll arrive by the tunnel the Jews escaped through. I don't want to risk being seen by the Germans who would then be asking awkward questions and possibly arrest me."

"I agree. I'll be waiting for you to let you in. Make sure you use the password we gave to the Jews so I know it's you and not the Germans especially as they must know about it by now having known where to look for the escaping Jews."

"I was actually going to use a different password just in case."

"Ok tell me what it is."

Marie, armed with the password went quietly to await Jean Paul. She looked around her to make sure there was no one waiting or watching, spying on her every move. This was becoming silly she thought. She'd become scared of her own shadow.

....

"Ok everyone, this is Jean Paul our resistance contact. He wants to speak to you all."

"Hi, you don't know me but I can assure you I can be trusted. I was helping with moving the Jews on. Unfortunately, before I became your contact there was a traitor, someone who was informing on the Jews you were hiding. It seems as if we got the wrong person...."

There were a few gasps of surprise at his statement. The nuns started murmuring amongst themselves, looking around at each other wondering who it could be.

"Can I have your attention again please ladies. One or more of you has a contact in the Gestapo."

"What?" exclaimed Marie.

"Yes, I didn't tell you but I was able to trace the source directly to a Gestapo officer."

"But surely none of us……"

"Yes one of you," cut in Jean Paul. His mouth was set in a firm line which warned Marie not to say anything further.

"I suspect one of you to be from Germany originally and the Gestapo officer is in fact your brother."

There were more gasps of surprise. They looked at each other suspiciously. Marie couldn't believe what she was hearing. None of them had a German accent. She also realised that with that much detail Jean Paul knew exactly who it was.

"I can't believe someone is in contact with family. It would be breaking our sacred vows."

"Nevertheless it is so," said Jean Paul.

"You know who it is don't you?" queried Marie.

Jean Paul nodded. "I'm hoping they'll own up without me having to drag it out of them."

There was silence as each one looked around wondering who it could be. Some looked decidedly nervous, worried that they might be in danger at that moment.

"Von Brandt is the name of the Gestapo contact. Is there anyone here with that name before taking your vows."

Again the group looked around but no one said anything.

"I'm sure there's some mistake," said Marie.

"Unfortunately not. Do I have to point out the person. Surely there isn't a coward in the room, realising your brother won't be able to help you now. You can't hide behind him any longer."

"This is too much I can't take it in. You must have your facts wrong."

"My source is very reliable. I am in charge here so don't question my judgement."

Marie looked suitably chastened, and was coming to recognise that Jean Paul might just be right. She looked around, half expecting to see a guilty look on the traitor's face or a mutinous expression, but saw nothing. They were all looking at each other mostly blank faces.

"Come on, make this easy for us. At least have the guts to own up and explain yourself," said Marie.

There was silence. Eve was starting to look frightened, worried she would get the blame not being a real nun and also the most recent addition to convent life. Some were starting to look at her, coming to that conclusion themselves.

"Why don't you own up?" said Monique. "Make it easy on the rest of us."

"It wasn't me," whispered Eve.

"It must have been. You're the only one we don't know about. You came professing to be a Jew but it doesn't mean you are. We took you under our wing and have protected you and this is how you repay us," said Claudette.

Eve began to cry. Not knowing how to prove herself innocent. It was as if she was being singled out and why not, she could understand where they were coming from. If she were one of them she would doubt herself as well.

"Come on everyone, calm down," said Marie. "I am sure Eve is telling the truth. We have already checked her out for she seemed the obvious one. Her background is exactly as she has described to us."

The talking and finger pointing stopped but Eve continued to get some dirty looks. She just hoped the real traitor would own up or be revealed as she couldn't take this any longer. She would rather be in the hands of the Germans than face this. Being disbelieved when she knew she was innocent of any wrongdoing was difficult to cope with.

Marie looked at Jean Paul with a questioning look. "Should we go back to my room and wait. Maybe the traitor would feel more able to own up if it wasn't in front of all of us.

"No," said Jean Paul with a shake of his head. "Everyone has to find out anyway so it should be in front of the whole community. It hasn't bothered the person that they have willingly spoken against you all. They should face the humiliation of everyone here."

"It's not humiliation, it's hatred," said Monique.

"Really," replied Jean Paul. "Is that how you feel?"

Monique nodded her head but stayed quiet.

"You should know," said Jean Paul.

Monique paled, "You're not suggesting it was me are you?"

"That's between you and your God. You know inside if you are the guilty one or not."

"I've had enough of this. I can't take anymore. You're accusing me of something I haven't done and I don't like it." Monique burst into tears and rushed out of the room.

"Now look what you've done," said Marie. "I'm going after her."

"Stay where you are. She'll be fine. She just likes amateur dramatics that's all. The tears will have stopped once she left here."

"You're not really trying to tell me it's Monique are you? She is one of the best. I confide in her when I need someone."

Jean Paul shrugged. "Do you believe it was her after the way she behaved when she left here."

Marie shook her head. "No. I think she was scared and alone, unsure what would happen next. I believe her. You must have made a mistake."

"But I haven't actually accused her of anything. It's just her reaction. Doesn't it make you consider that this could be the reaction of a guilty person."

"Not really," said Marie.

"What about you Claudette, isn't that your name?"

"Yes, but I am innocent it wasn't me. I know that's hard to believe as I'm relatively new here"

"You're telling the truth," said Jean Paul.

Claudette breathed a sigh of relief, glad to know she was off the hook. She started to think in her mind that Jean Paul was suspicious of Monique. Certainly her reaction was that of someone who was guilty or innocent.

Chapter Twenty One

The first thing Marie knew was the shouting. She sat up in bed and listened. She could be imagining it but doubted it. It sounded like German. Had they finally come for them, alerted no doubt by the traitor who would be frightened and anxious at the thought of being exposed. Which was close to happening now that Jean Paul knew who it was. She was surprised that he hadn't revealed it the previous evening when he turned up to speak to everyone about the situation.

She got up and looked out the window to find everywhere still dark. It must be the middle of the night, thought Marie, although that was inconsequential if the Germans were going to take them all in. Would they take the sister of the Gestapo officer? Maybe this was the way they would get discovered if the Germans treated her better than the rest of them. It would cease to matter then of course but it would be nice to know who it was and why. All the nuns had been at the convent long before the invasion so surely she hadn't been planted there to spy on what they get up to. Also there was nothing to suggest they would be involved in hiding Jews so what was the motive?

Marie was finding herself more and more suspicious of the nuns underneath her. She kept thinking if she watched closely she would see one give themselves away somehow. It hadn't happened yet if anything all the nuns were acting peculiarly, obviously feeling self conscious and worrying that they would be accused if they weren't careful even though innocent.

"Come on up now," cried a German bursting into Marie's room.

"Can I please get dressed?" she asked politely. "I can't possibly go anywhere without looking like a nun and neither can the others."

The German gave a brief nod and turned his back. No way was he leaving anyone alone in case they sent out some sort of coded message for help. He didn't want the whole of the resistance descending on them.   There wouldn't be enough lorries to round up the nuns and the rogues from outside unless he shot the lot of them that was.

Marie was dragged out of her room before she could get her habit straight. She was met by other terrified nuns in the entrance hall. She tried to speak but was told to shut up and slapped around the face.

"There is no need for violence, we are peaceful people and will go with you and obey your orders."

"Shut up. Didn't you get the message the first time." This time she was hit around the head with the gun. She almost slipped to the floor but was prevented from doing so by the Germans holding her up one on each side.

There were a few gasps from those around who had just witnessed the brutality which was unnecessary in their opinion. They didn't like their Reverend Mother being abused in this way. Some were taken by surprise, not believing that the enemy could treat them like that. They were used to respect and civilised behaviour not being treated like animals or worse than animals.

Marie watched closely as the rest of the convent crowded into the small space. No one seemed to stand out as being involved with the Germans. Was it possible that Jean Paul had got it wrong, although she couldn't see how. The resistance had so many contacts they could easily find the correct information with ease.

Obviously for now at least the traitor was being treated in the same rough way as all of them. She'd find out more soon she was sure. She was aware that the traitor wouldn't make it obvious but might be in communication with the Germans in subtle ways.

They were taken out and loaded on the lorries watched by neighbours who were nose twitching from their own homes. They daren't attempt to go out while the Germans were taking away the inhabitants of the convent. If they were to go outside they might get caught up in it all and end up packed off to goodness knows where not knowing if they would survive.

Marie and Monique were sitting together which they had manipulated so they could discuss the matter. They needed to hold up and not let the others know how afraid they really were.

"Hopefully wherever they take us we'll be able to be together," said Marie.

"Don't hold your breath on that one."

"Why?"

"Because you can bet they'll not let people be together. They won't want us to create a mini convent from the camp."

"I suppose you're right. I had been thinking along those lines anyway."

"Somehow we need to encourage everyone, keep them strong in the knowledge that Our Lady will intervene for us. When the war is over and the Nazis gone we can go back to our convent and start again."

"If it's still there you mean. We have no way of knowing what will happen to it now. The Germans might take it for their use and that will destroy it for us especially the chapel. I can't see it remaining intact. I'd still like to know who amongst us is a traitor. If it hadn't been for their interference we might still be living in peace behind those walls," said Marie.

"You don't know that. We would probably still face this at some point even if it was in the future."

"You're probably right but I still need to know. They can't be allowed to continue as a nun."

"I still have to disagree, I don't see it's relevance now."

Marie stopped the conversation which was going nowhere and looked around at the others. She noticed Eve very pale, holding herself rigid and shaking.

Marie leaned across and spoke in a whisper, "It's going to be ok. If we are together we'll all look out for you. They'll never know the truth about your identity."

"But what about the traitor? They know so could inform on me at some point."

"Let's hope and pray they don't. I don't think they'll achieve anything by doing so not anymore."

"Out of pure malice they could," whispered Eve.

"It's possible," said Marie feeling very reluctant. She didn't like to think of any of the nuns behaving in that way, but then she never believed they would reach out to the enemy as they had done.

"Come on you lot out now," shouted one of the Germans.

Marie looked around as she jumped out, nearly tripping over on the loose stones on the ground. They were at a railway station with what looked like cattle trucks stood waiting. Waiting for what, she wondered. She never believed they were for them until she saw others getting on further down the line. Sure enough they were roughly pushed into one of them. This is too much, she thought to herself. She felt herself start shaking just like Eve had been. This was frightening. Where were they going to end up? Surely they wouldn't be taken to one of the camps like the Jews that she had heard about from Jacques. Jean Paul had never mentioned them but then he didn't need to. She had been involved with the resistance group that were responsible for hiding Jews and helping them escape France.

They didn't have to wait long before they were on the move again. The trucks had small slats along the side of the trucks allowing them to see out, even if the view was limited. They were going quite slowly and occasionally showed signs of slowing down but they never came to a complete standstill.

The truck the nuns were in was full to bursting. There wasn't even room to sit on the floor of the truck. It wasn't just the nuns but others as well. Marie wanted to find out if any of the others knew what might be going to happen.

She tried talking to the woman she found herself next to but she was sullen and refused to speak except for a load of vitriol against the Germans. Marie was never going to get sense out of her that was obvious.

Monique, too, was trying to talk to one of the other women but just got a shrug of the shoulders. No one seemed inclined to talk but many looked scared to death.

Marie, looking around, decided it was up to her to keep morale up. She decided to try singing to see if others would join in. It was only what they sang in chapel but was soothing and might bring peace to everyone. The other nuns joined in and even Eve started to sing and some of the pallor left her which Marie was pleased to see. The others in their listening to the nuns singing found a sense of peace which they couldn't explain filling themselves and the truck. They sang one song after another until they got tired and slowly one by one fell silent until Marie and Monique were singing on their own.

They soon came to a full stop. The sides were opened and they were herded out. Marie was surprised to see the sun shining brightly and beaming down warmth on them. It had been chilly in the truck.

They were ordered to walk following a couple of soldiers. Anyone falling behind was beaten by the Germans and left for dead on the ground. Fortunately all the nuns were in good health and were able to keep up easily.

After what seemed like an eternity they came to some large iron gates. They opened and the group of women entered. They were stopped once inside. Looking around there were what looked like a dozen wooden huts. All surrounded by barbed wire which was high. There were also guards towers dotted around the edge of the camp with a German sitting in each holding a gun, ready to shoot if necessary.

Marie was happy to see that all her nuns were congregated in one hut which already seemed over full of prisoners. Marie tried asking questions but no one was prepared to tell them anything. The nuns were just going to have to follow the lead of those already there to avoid breaking rules.

A whistle blew, the door of their hut was pushed open and the German guards herded the new inmates out and into lines. In front of them stood a young man. Eyes ice blew and cruel, at least that was how Marie interpreted them with a shiver.

"Hello," said the German in that language.

It was then interpreted by a French prisoner who obviously spoke fluent German. Marie realised that for one of her nuns would be understanding perfectly well. She wished she knew who it was but couldn't look around as they had to keep their eyes to the front on the German who was describing the rules and regulations and the daily routine they were all to follow. Anyone caught breaking any of these would be severely punished. They were expected to work hard for the German masters. Again

Marie thought of the frailer nuns who might find it difficult. The convent life was kept simple and those who were unable to cope with physical labour were given simpler tasks to do, such as collecting eggs from the hens they kept.

They were allowed back to their hut when they were finished. Marie hoped to find out more about coping with physical labour from those who had been there a while.

"You're having a laugh right?" said one of the prisoners. "There is no letting up we have to manage as best we can. Don't let them see you're struggling or you're for it. Anyway can't you ask your God to save you from this hell," she added disdainfully.

"Sorry, didn't mean to cause offence," said Marie, totally out of her depth with this lady.

"Yeah right!"

"Take no notice of her," called out another lady. "I'm Veronique. We try and help each other without letting the guards see. We have to protect our own as we are all the same here."

"Marie. Nice to meet you."

Veronique smiled shyly and Marie felt she may have made a friend. In normal circumstances particular friendships were frowned upon but she felt in this instance this rule could be broken. Marie approached Veronique and they chatted more about conditions in the camp and the guards. Marie learned that there was one guard who turned a blind eye to some things. Marie felt hopeful that they would survive this horror with friends like Veronique. She learned that Jeanne was the name of the unfriendly lady who had scoffed at Marie and her questions.

At least that was one person to avoid. Marie felt sorry for her as she must be so bitter to talk like that, but who knew what she had been through before landing in the camp. She would probably never know as it was unlikely she'd be met with civility from her.

Eve sat on her bunk shivering. She didn't know what was wrong she just could not stop. She wrapped the coarse, rough blanket around herself in an effort to keep warm but it didn't help just irritated her sensitive skin.

"Hey, are you ok?" asked Monique who had been looking around with interest.

"I don't know. I can't stop shivering."

"Probably shock," said Monique, who knew enough first aid to know this.

"I'm so scared," said Eve.

"We all are," said Monique.

"But what if they find out who I am?"

"There's no reason why they should," responded Monique, trying to sound more certain than she was.

"Who are you? Some royal princess?" asked Jeanne. "You won't get any special favours here whoever you maybe. We're all the same prisoners of the Third Reich."

"Keep out of it," said Monique. "Her situation is nothing to do with you."

"Isn't it? If she wants to be treated differently she won't get it here. "

"Why do you have to be so nasty?" asked Monique.

"Monique, stop that," said a horrified Marie, who still felt she had some control over the nuns.

Monique subsided automatically obeying their leader.

Marie was relieved as she felt before long any control she had would be stripped away as they continued to try and fit in with the rest.

"That's right do as you're told," scoffed Jeanne.

Marie gave a slight shake of her head that only Monique could see. It was enough to prevent her from replying.

"We're never going to cope with this," said Monique in a whisper, not wanting Jeanne to hear and come back with some insult.

"We have no choice unfortunately. We are here through no fault of our own. We were only doing God's work. Somehow we have to fit in and do what we are told. We know that our Lady is interceding at all times."

"I suppose so. It's come as quite a shock though. We are just not used to this."

"Maybe not but we must make the best of it and show the others a new way of behaving. We must be submissive to the Germans I believe just as we submit to God. It goes against everything but it's for the best."

"I know, but it's so hard. I just wonder how some of the younger nuns will cope with what may seem like freedom from all the routine of convent life."

"We have to be strong and show them the way."

Monique nodded but inside she wasn't so sure. In some ways she was looking forward to a new routine however brutal. It surely couldn't be as restrictive as convent life. She intended in fully embracing this new way of living.

Marie saw a look on Monique's face and knew she could lose her if she didn't handle this carefully and wisely. There was something in Monique's face she couldn't recognise but made her give an involuntary shiver. Thoughts came unbidden into her mind which she tried to dismiss but couldn't quite manage it. Surely she was wrong. She couldn't be right. She couldn't get the thought out of her mind though. She sincerely hoped she was wrong but something wasn't right here. Could it really be? She had always trusted and confided in Monique but was that misplaced? She always had Monique marked as her successor should she ever become incapable to be the Reverend Mother. Now she was having other thoughts. It was all coming out now and she was seeing the real Monique and she didn't like what she was seeing. If only Jean Paul were around to advise. He could offer an opinion and even tell her if her thoughts were going along the right lines since he knew who it was. He could just give a yes or no answer or not answer at all which would also be an answer in the affirmative.

Marie was certain in her own mind but knew she needed to keep it to herself for the moment. She would have to wait for the right moment if that were to ever come. She felt her eyes grow heavy and allowed them to close and slip into an unrefreshing sleep full of nightmares.

Chapter Twenty Two

A noise blared out waking even the deepest slumber. Everyone seemed to be getting up quickly so the nuns followed suit.

"Come on, we have to get out it's roll call now. We have to line up just as you did yesterday on arrival," said Veronique to the nuns.

Very quickly all were in place looking directly towards the front and the commandant.

Marie could feel it was going to be a warm day although the sun wasn't even up yet it was so early. She had learned from Veronique that this could happen at any time depending on how sadistic the guards were feeling and also if the prisoners had obeyed the rules made a difference.

She tried to look around her at her fellow nuns without making it obvious what she was doing. She failed however as a booming voice called her out to the front.

She went knowing that Jeanne was glaring at her for keeping them there longer than necessary. Reluctantly she stood before the commandant, not knowing what would happen next and if she were to admit it just a bit frightened. She was supposed to be setting an example to the nuns under her but here she was in trouble.

"Right," said the interpreter, "Lift your clothes up and bend over slightly."

"I can't do that," said Marie quietly.

A collective gasp went around the camp at the audacity of speaking like that to their captors.

"You will do as you are told." The commandant was not going to let her get away with anything. She had to follow the rules like everyone else and submit to any punishment they saw fit to impose.

Marie shook her head. The commandant slapped her hard around the face. Still she refused to do so. Another hard slap, this time it nearly sent her tumbling to the ground but she managed to stay upright.

"Get on the ground," roared the commandant.

Marie reluctantly obeyed this request. She got down on her knees. The commandant forced her clothes up around her leaving a bare back. Tears poured down her face as she faced the indignity. What sort of impression would this give some of the younger nuns seeing their leader so humiliated.

The commandant picked the whip up which was on the ground and began striking Marie hard across the back. She flinched at every blow but was determined to stay strong and not cry out. They got harder causing a whimper as she felt the lashes strike her. She felt everything start to go black before fading into unconsciousness. The commandant stopped and with a fierce look faced the rest.

"This is what will happen if you disobey. You will at all times face me, not looking down, or to the sides. Dismissed."

Monique rushed forward to Marie but was pushed away with the commandant's gun. "She stays where she is as an example to you all."

Everyone, including the old hands at prison camp life, looked aghast at Marie. They had never seen anyone receive such a severe beating. Some like Jeanne couldn't help thinking it was her own fault but most were sympathetic, knowing how it could so easily be them next time They had witnessed the cruelty of the camp guards.

Eve was in tears bringing Jeanne's wrath down on her. "It's her own fault and now we're going to bear the brunt of their anger for the rest of the day. They will be harder on us, so dry up. There is no room for wimpish behaviour."

"Don't speak to her like that," said Veronique. "I'm sure you were the same when you first arrived."

"I should hope not."

Veronique shook her head, not wanting to get into an argument. Jeanne was a hard case. Veronique didn't know if it was the camp or her previous life that had made her that way.

Monique put her arms around Eve to try and bring some comfort to her. Eve was especially upset as she had received so much kindness and help from Marie whilst at the convent and to see her so tortured was unbearable.

Eve slowly stopped and wiped her swollen eyes.

"Feeling better," asked Monique.

Eve nodded but still unable to speak.

"I hope you're not going to turn on the waterworks every time something like that happens or you'll be a permanent dripping tap. There is always something they are not happy with," said Jeanne, disgust written all over her face.

"That's uncalled for," said Veronique.

"I don't think so. We don't want someone like that in here. Not good for morale."

"Oh shut up," said Monique, unable to keep her mouth shut but knowing that Marie wouldn't like her getting involved.

"Who's going to make me?" asked Jeanne, ready for a fight.

"Stop it at once the pair of you," said Veronique. "We don't need to bring the guards down on us because of you two."

Jeanne ignored her and launched herself at Monique, who not expecting this was knocked to the ground. Jeanne felt on top of her and rained blows down on her.

Veronique and a couple of others tried pulling Jeanne away to no avail. She was strong and beyond common sense at that point. She ignored the shouts of the rest of the hut trying to stop her beating Monique to a pulp.

When Monique stopped struggling Jeanne stopped and got off her. Monique was in a bad way anyone could see that. Her face was swollen and her nose bleeding. It looked as if her nose was broken as it didn't look completely straight, but was hard to tell amongst the general puffiness.

"Come on you lot," said a guard bursting in.

A few of them quickly gathered around Monique not wanting her to be seen and bring more wrath down on their heads.

"You really shouldn't have done that," said Veronique.

Jeanne shrugged, "She asked for it."

"You didn't have to be so brutal about it. You could get us all into trouble. You know they don't like it if fighting breaks out. It means less of a workforce for them."

Jeanne looked as if she couldn't care less and didn't bother to respond but turned away to make her way out of the hut. Veronique shook her head, Jeanne was a loose cannon and they were walking on egg shells all the time to avoid problems. No one liked her or got on with her. It could have been hoped that she would calm down a bit with the presence of the nuns but if anything it made her worse.

As they all left the hut for breakfast Eve noticed Marie stirring. She rushed over to her to see if she needed any help. She had a soft spot for Marie who had so readily taken her and Francesca and shielded them so well.

Marie sort of opened her eyes into slits.

"Are you all right?" asked Eve.

Marie made no response which worried Eve as she was definitely awake. Veronique came rushing over. "Come on Eve you can't be seen hanging around here or you'll be next. I know it's not right but we just have to get on with it. You'll see enough beatings here but you must ignore them."

Eve made no attempt to move away until Veronique grabbed her arm and pulled her away.

"You don't understand, she's done so much to help me."

"That's as maybe but you can't stay here. Hey don't cry," she said seeing the tears well up in Eve's eyes.

"You don't understand. She took me in and let me masquerade as a nun just to keep….." Eve gasped as she realised she'd said more than she should.

"You're not a nun?"

Eve shook her head. "I'm a Jew. My husband got taken and me and Francesca reached the convent and got hidden there until it became unsafe to stay there any longer. Francesca was with another lady and child that got taken while they were escaping. I avoided it by reaching the safety of the convent again."

"You're a Jew. I would never have guessed."

"Please, I've said too much," said Eve with a flicker of fear crossing her face.

"Don't worry you're safe with me, but please don't repeat this story to anyone as you don't know who you can trust. Someone could easily tell the guards and that would be it for you."

Eve nodded. She had no intention of telling anyone and certainly hadn't thought of telling Veronique. She would be more guarded in what she said in future. Hints and direct speaking were out of the question for her.

Chapter Twenty Three

"You know, there is something strange about Eve. She doesn't act like the rest of the nuns," said Jeanne to Paulette who was the closest to a friend that Jeanne had.

"Doesn't she? I hadn't noticed any difference really."

"Open your eyes then you'll see what I see."

Paulette decided to keep an eye out. She was a gossip and this could be a nice juicy bit for them to mull over. She was also a favourite with the Germans, ready to pass anything exciting to them and she sensed a story here. It might help her win more favours with their captors.

"Thank you Jeanne. I'll keep a look out and see what I can find out."

Jeanne went on her way happy with what she had achieved. She noticed there was something odd about Eve and wanted to know what it was. She had a malicious streak in her and wouldn't hesitate to tell someone in authority if there was anything to say. This time it might be safer to pass the information on to Paulette and leave it to her to sort out. Jeanne was a coward inside and didn't want to be the one to pass that titbit on. She was prepared to leave it to Paulette to tell and then face the wrath of the hut.

"Be careful," whispered Veronique who had become a firm friend of Eve. "I think Jeanne is on to you and she's said something to Paulette as well."

"Oh no, I feel sick. How could anyone have guessed."

"Anyone with eyes could see what is straight in front of them." There was compassion in Veronique's eyes and her words. She really wanted Eve to stay on the right side of the guards and other inmates. Eve, when you got to know her was a lot of fun and had a strong sense of humour which had survived the loss of her family and known such fear in hiding. Veronique really admired this in Eve. She must be such a strong person to keep that essential part of her personality.

"What are you two talking about?" asked Monique, approaching them.

"Not a lot," said Veronique immediately.

Monique's face had finally healed from the beating but still had a bit of swelling around her nose. Marie, too was getting better although she would bear the scars for life, not just the physical but psychological as well. She had become wary of anyone and was no longer the strong leader she had once been. It was sad to those who knew her to see this happen, knowing that if they survived and were allowed back to the convent she might never be able to lead them again. She had become withdrawn and rarely spoke now. Broken beyond repair.

They had been their a few weeks by this time and they were all changing. They no longer were as trusting as they had been, much more aware of the current evil in the world than they had been when living isolated in the convent. They were aware that anyone could tell tales just to see them get punished so stayed as silent and aloof as possible with the exception of Eve who was becoming close to Veronique. She wasn't disobeying any rules as she hadn't taken her vows and never would. Posing as a Catholic nun was tricky when she just wanted to be like the other prisoners.

Veronique knew about the traitor in their midst and had her own ideas as to who it was, based on her own observations. She wasn't saying though. She knew when to keep things to herself. If it was so obvious to her she couldn't believe none of the nuns had noticed. She supposed it must be because they were very naïve about the workings of this world. In some ways she envied them, sometimes it would be nice to live in a little bubble, that way she could avoid being hurt or hurting at the situation in the world with all that was going on around her.

No one ever spoke of the end of the war and being freed. It seemed like an impossible dream which would never come true. They didn't know what was happening in the outside world, which was nothing new to the nuns. The Germans gave them updates but no one believed them knowing them for the propaganda they were.

Chapter Twenty Four

They were all stood around at role call. They were hugging themselves in the freezing cold weather. The sky looked ominous. Some of the prisoners were aware it could snow and quaked inside. It would make their work doubly hard if they were working through snow. The Germans wouldn't let them have a day off because of it. All that would happen was the beatings would get worse.

The cold weather was starting to cause ill health amongst the frailer prisoners, but still the Germans drove them on until they dropped. No humane treatment from them.

The women were trying not to stamp their freezing numb feet, knowing they would be beaten within an inch of their life if they so much as moved. The Germans were keeping them standing longer than usual and some believed it to be deliberate.

"Ok, I have some news for you. We are getting ready to invade Great Britain," announced the commandant.

There was a collective gasp around the women.

"Silence!" he yelled, unwilling to allow even that sound from them.

Some prisoners looked sceptical but many especially the nuns believed him, not having it in them to think anyone could lie just to dent their morale and make them think they were losing the war.

Seeing Eve looking frightened, Veronique gave a slight shake of her head. Eve caught the meaning and relaxed slightly. Veronique was used to such announcements and generally ignored them. It was the best way.

Finally they were allowed to go back to their huts, prepare for work.

"You don't need to panic too much Eve," said Veronique, "I doubt it's true. They like giving out such propaganda to make it look as if the allies are losing the war. It makes them look good and makes us more subservient to them. It's a good way of keeping control of us."

"I suppose you could be right," conceded Eve.

"I know I am," said Veronique.

Eve sighed. "It's just so hard and I miss my little girl."

Paulette passing them at that moment, pricked up her ears. Little girl, but she was a nun. This was some scandal she was sure of it. She now knew what Jeanne meant.

Veronique noticing whispered to Eve to be quiet about such things as there were people around who wouldn't think twice but to tell on her.

Paulette having heard all she needed to, stored it at the back of her mind to mull over and discuss the situation with Jeanne.

"So I'm right," said Jeanne feeling very satisfied with herself. "A daughter, well that really does speak volumes. Nuns don't have children."

"What if she isn't even a nun?" queried Paulette.

"I don't think she is, considering the way she is building a friendship with Veronique. The other nuns remain aloof, not attempting to get to know any of us."

"Why say she's a nun if she isn't?"

"I don't know, we need to find out more, although I don't know how we'll get the information. No one will talk to us and trying to get anywhere will just put Eve on her guard and we'll never know anything for sure."

"We just wait and keep eyes and ears open then," said Paulette.

Jeanne nodded with a faraway look in her eyes. She was thinking and coming up with possible answers. Ones which would make juicy bits of gossip and surely it would get back to the Germans. A malicious smile appeared on her face making even Paulette shiver. She wondered if it was a good idea to continue. She liked a gossip and to be in favour with the guards but she didn't want any one to come to harm and she sensed that it could happen if the truth ever came to light about Eve. She surprised herself by feeling a bit protective of Eve. It wasn't like her but she wasn't like Jeanne either. She knew Jeanne used her and she had allowed that up until now.

....

"Oh dear, I ache all over," said Eve.

"Are you not well?" asked Veronique who was with her as usual. The two really were becoming inseparable.

"I don't know. It might just be the awful back breaking work. Those boulders are so heavy and make worse when we have to dig them out of the snow first before we attempt to move them."

Veronique nodded in understanding. They were all struggling and two prisoners had already died. The snow had been around for a couple of weeks and they were all tired of it. In reality they should have a bit of leeway due to the weather but to suggest it would bring down the wrath of the Germans on their heads. They would possibly all be punished for it.

"At least here you're relatively safe, compared to where you could be."

Jeanne again, passing by slowed down to see if she could find out anymore before they realised she was nearby and listening. She stealthily moved a bit closer but didn't dare go further as she would almost be breathing down their necks and that would alert them. She was so sure she was near to finding out what was really going on. If she couldn't she was quite prepared to make something up just to tell Paulette, whom she could sense was withdrawing from her.

Paulette had been doing a lot of thinking about herself and was not liking what she saw. She realised why people ignored her and definitely wanted to change. Previously so friendly with Jeanne but now not wanting to be drawn into gossip to curry favour with the Germans. She envied the friendship between Eve and Veronique and the nuns with their quiet ways. She hoped it wasn't too late to change. Would any of the prisoners believe it though. She knew if she had any gossip on Eve she would ignore it. She was sure Eve had been through a lot in spite of her sense of humour and willingness to have a laugh. There was her daughter wherever she was. She must miss her. She didn't know why they weren't together but didn't want to know, then Jeanne wouldn't be able to taunt her with it.

She started to withdraw seeing Jeanne approach.

"You know I think Eve's a Jew," said Jeanne with a smile.

"I don't care," said Paulette trying to move away.

Jeanne followed her, "Don't walk away from me or you'll get it."

"Do what you like," said Paulette more bravely than she felt. Although realising at the same time that it might be better for her if Jeanne were to beat her up. It might change the reputation she had with the others.

"Don't think it will help you if you ignore gossip. I could still tell the guards and make out it came from you when retribution falls."

"Do what you like, but I know it won't be me and that's the main thing. My conscience will be clear."

Jeanne didn't like the way the conversation was going. It seemed to her that she had lost control of Paulette which would leave her alone and friendless.

She made one last attempt to get Paulette back in her shadow. "Look, if you don't do as I say I could tell them you're really a Jew then they'll do what they like with you."

Paulette felt a piercing dart through her whole body at this but she refused to give Jeanne the satisfaction of knowing she had been scared by it. She was determined to get away from Jeanne once and for all.

"Do your worst," she said.

Jeanne gave up realising that anything she did would not affect Paulette who no longer cared.

Paulette tried to show she had changed by trying to have friendly conversations with the others, without digging for any gossip. It was an uphill job as everyone automatically moved away from her when she approached and wouldn't respond if she said anything.

Eve and Veronique, who by now were inseparable, discussed the situation.

"You know, I wonder if we should be giving her a chance," suggested Eve.

"I don't know if it's worth the risk. We don't want her to realise who you really are and tell the guards."

"I don't think she will. She's going out of her way to avoid Jeanne and is trying to be friendly. If we respond then maybe the others will follow. Of course we have to be careful what we say but she might be on the level."

"You know I think you've spent too long with the nuns."

Eve laughed, "You could be right but I still think she should have the benefit of the doubt here."

Veronique thought for a moment then nodded in agreement.

Next time Paulette approached they went out of their way to be nice to her without saying too much. Paulette was surprised but hopeful that they might be starting to come around to her.

Eve and Veronique started including Paulette in their conversations and the duo soon became a threesome. The other prisoners seeing this started responding to Paulette as well. Jeanne watched this with jealousy. She had no one and didn't know how to change that. She was so hard and bitter she didn't know how to change even if she wanted to.

Jeanne noticed she no longer had the power over the prisoners as more and more they were deliberately saying things to her which before would have made her lash out. They were no longer frightened of her and this she hated. She enjoyed the sense of power it gave her. She thought about going to the guards with information but realised it would only set the women more against her. She was worried if anything were to happen they might surge toward her and as a group beat her up instead of the other way around. Of course it was Paulette she blamed for this state of affairs. How she'd love to break up the trio that were now so close.

. . . .

Marie watched silently from her own little world. She was pleased to see Eve making good friends even if it caused suspicion over whether she was a real nun. Although she said nothing to anyone she had completely lost all her faith. She had completely relinquished any leadership she had. She no longer saw herself as the Reverend Mother. She was just like the other prisoners. The other nuns had noticed and automatically looked to Monique as their leader. Monique had tried to talk to Marie but got nowhere so Monique took up the role with enthusiasm. She hoped when they were released Marie might come back to herself and take over once again.

Chapter Twenty Five

They were all stood around during yet another role call when suddenly the sky was filled with planes. The women looked up and seeing allied planes cheered and waved their arms. The commandant shouted at them to try and get back control but to no avail. He threatened punishments but they took no notice.

The planes were flying surprisingly low. Suddenly bombs started dropping nearby. The women screamed and ran for cover, totally forgetting they were at role call and should obey the commandant. He continued standing there with the other guards furious that his authority had been ignored. He would have to take control back and after some thought knew how he would do it. The women would be sorry they had ignored his bidding.

The planes disappeared without any of the bombs falling on the camp. It was enough to give the women hope of release very soon and the end of the war which would follow. For all they knew the war could have already finished since allied planes were flying overhead. Veronique, sensible as always, pointed out if the war had ended bombs wouldn't have fallen. The women calmed down, their enthusiasm dampened for the moment. The sound to role call again reminded them they had forgotten they had been there when the planes appeared. A few looked worried, sure there would be repercussions. This was borne out when they lined up and looked at the furious face of the commandant.

"You know of course there must be punishment for your terrible behaviour earlier," he said. "You will line up in front of me and approach one at a time."

Some of the women almost fainted as they realised what was to come. Others felt it was worth it as they had a hint of freedom which could be fast approaching. This was the first time allied planes had been spotted.

Lining up they approached and got a sound whipping. The women tried not to make a sound as they didn't want to make things worse for themselves.

"You shouldn't be whipping me," cried Jeanne when it came to her turn. "Look to those amongst us who are Jews."

The women all gasped as she said this. Eve and her two friends, Veronique and Paulette, looked at each other. Was Jeanne going to give Eve away?

The commandant halted as the whip was about to land on Jeanne's back.

"You better be telling me the truth or this will be worse for you."

"I am sir," said Jeanne.

"Ok," roared the commandant. "Which of you are Jews? Step forward now."

There was a deathly silence over the camp. No one spoke up, some began to look frightened, worried they might be accused of being Jews. Others looked around wondering who

Jeanne was talking about. Some eyes looked pointedly at Paulette thinking it must be her as she had once been close with Jeanne and the only one that Jeanne knew best.

"Come on I can't wait. If this lady is telling the truth I mean to find out who you are. Or I could call the Gestapo in to help and that you won't like believe me. Of course I could hand you all over saying I've just discovered you're all Jews and let you be taken. Your chances of survival will be zero I can assure you of that."

No one moved. Paulette put her hand up and moved forward, eyes on the ground. "I am sir," she whispered.

"Speak up lady. What are you?"

"A Jew sir."

Jeanne dared to turn round and look at Paulette in surprise. She was well aware that Paulette was not a Jew so why would she say she was?

Jeanne spoke now, "She's not a Jew. She's covering for someone."

Paulette paled. She didn't want Eve to be discovered. She would rather accept what was coming. She didn't know why she should feel this way. She had no faith to speak of so had no reason other than friendship to protect Eve.

"Which of you is telling the truth?"

"I am sir," they said in unison.

"You can't both be."

"It's true sir, it's me," said Paulette.

Veronique looked at Eve and stepped forward. Eve held her breath, worried for the first time that maybe her friend might be going to tell on her. She was too much of a coward to own up herself which she should have at the beginning. Was she wrong to have trusted Veronique?

"Sir, they are both lying. The Jew is Jeanne who is before you and pretending it's not her."

Everyone startled at hearing this, looked around at each other wondering if this could be true. All they really knew at this point was that someone in their midst was a Jew. Was that why Jeanne had set herself apart from them all and was so nasty because she didn't want to be uncovered for who she really was?

Eve stepped forward about to admit the truth but Monique grabbed her and pulled her back. "Don't," she whispered.

Eve raised her eyebrows questioningly.

"Save yourself. Also don't forget you're here as a nun so don't put us all in jeopardy by stating the truth. We'd all be punished for hiding you."

Eve stopped in her tracks realising the truth of this. She certainly didn't want to get the nuns or anyone else in trouble. The nuns had done so much for her and Francesca as well as the other Jews they'd helped.

The commandant looked again at Jeanne. "Well I suppose you have the look of a Jew."

Jeanne, pale and shaking, tried denying it but the commandant decided to believe Veronique. He looked across at

Eve and called her to the front. "What was it you were going to say before you were pulled back?"

"I was going to agree with Veronique. The Jew is Jeanne."

Monique let out a sigh of relief. She had been worried for a moment that Eve would tell the truth. She knew Eve to be very truthful and had never been caught out in a lie. She was also very loyal and it was that loyalty that kept her from getting the nuns into trouble as well.

The commandant looked again at Jeanne with a look of disgust on his face. "A filthy Jew then. I don't know why we didn't see this to begin with. Now we know I have to think what to do with you. I could hand you over to the Gestapo or I could take matters into my own hands and save them a job. I don't know whether you would be sent to one of the camps for Jews or whether they would torture and kill you instead."

"Please it really isn't me," said Jeanne. "I'm a Catholic although a lapsed one."

"That's a downright lie," cried Paulette forgetting where she was, so incensed by the lie as she was. "You are not a Catholic and have never been or you wouldn't have ridiculed the nuns when they arrived in the way that you did."

"If that's a lie then we can not believe you when you say you are not a Jew. I think I should make an example of you right here," said the commandant, so full of rage as he was.

"Stand up straight."

He began whipping Jeanne badly before passing it to the other guards to each have their turn.

Just as she was about to pass out he turned his gun on her, pointing at her head.

Eve turned away, not being able to watch what should have been happening to her. This wasn't right, she couldn't let it continue but Monique held on to her refusing to let her reveal the truth.

BANG!!! The shot rang out. Jeanne fell to the ground, blood pouring from her ear and her mouth. She twitched before falling unconscious. Just to be certain she was dead he pointed the gun at her again and opened fire.

Eve covered her ears unable to bear what had just happened.

Even worse was to come.

"Come closer," said the commandant to Paulette. "I don't appreciate people lying to me. I don't know why you would want to cover for a filthy Jew but you must be punished as well. He lifted his gun and pointed it at her head.

Eve screamed. Monique covered her mouth, wanting to muffle the sound. The last thing she wanted was to bring the commandant's attention to Eve and then for him to find out the truth.

The noise of the gun rang out again. The sound was deafening and many of the women were by now covering their ears, not being able to cope with the noise or the sight of one of their own being shot just as an example to them all.

Eve looked at the two dead women laying on the ground blood soaking into the earth.

The commandant turned to the rest and commanded them to move the bodies and take them to where the guards asked. They were to dig a deep hole in which the two women were to be thrown. This would be on the outskirts of the camp but still just inside the boundary.

Eve started vomiting as they did as they were bidden. All she got was a slap around her face from a guard.

After the bodies had been buried they were sent to their jobs. There was nothing easy about their daily tasks. It was back breaking work. They were expected to move heavy boulders on their own and carry them to the other side of the camp and build them up. No one knew what the purpose of this was or whether it was just something made up to give them something to do that would break them.

On this particular day they were worked harder than ever on the commands of the commandant again. He was really punishing them more than ever because of the fiasco that had taken place.

Eve could barely function. In her mind she was reliving what had happened. The guilt was almost too much to bear. It should have been her not Jeanne or Paulette. She wished Monique hadn't held her back and then it would have been her and others lives would have been spared.

Every now and again tears slid down her cheeks. She was especially devastated by the loss of her friend. She hadn't been friends with Paulette for long but it was enough. She had been part of Eve's and Veronique's little group.

She stopped and sniffed.

"Get back to work. Or do you want to face the same thing your friends did."

Eve shook her head glumly. She couldn't even foresee a time when she would be happy again. Having lost her family, she had now lost her friend.

Veronique seeing this approached her. "Come on keep going. We'll chat later. I know and understand that this must be very hard for you when you know it should have been you on the receiving end of those bullets. I've lost a friend as well. We'll grieve together and have a chat later back in the hut."

Eve nodded but said nothing. Veronique patted her on the back and moved away before a guard noticed anything amiss.

It started getting dark but still the women were made to work on. They were all showing signs of flagging now. One or two of the strongest ones were ok but most were half dead with exhaustion and their muscles giving up.

One of the women fell over and a guard literally dragged her to her feet and held her as each guard whipped her to within an inch of her life. Eve and Veronique looked at each other and grimaced. They were all facing punishment for the events that had taken place that day. How much longer must they be made to work like this.

It was soon pitch dark and yet the women were still working. More were collapsing unable to go on any longer. Each were whipped and forced to carry on. So the punishment continued. They hadn't had any food or drink that day which was also taking its toll. The quality and quantity of food left much to be desired but at least it was something which was better than a completely empty stomach.

"I don't think I can go on much longer," whispered Eve to Veronique when she had a chance.

"Nor me, but we have to keep going. We have no choice unless we want to risk being killed as well."

Still they were forced to continue this back breaking work. No stops to rest their weary bodies, no food, no drink, just hard labour.

Just as Eve was about to drop unable to stay upright any longer the call to role call broke the silence. Eve was not the only one who sighed with relief.

They staggered to the square and attempted to stand upright looking at the commandant. "Well I hope you've learned your lesson. I will not be disobeyed. I don't care what else is going on you carry on as normal. You do not deviate from routine unless instructed to do so by us."

There was silence. No one dared say anything they were just glad it was over, or was it. The commandant stayed there watching the women closely. He was looking for signs of weakness, hoping to punish further any who couldn't stand still. They already knew he came across as a sadist but this was too much. There were many, including Eve who just wanted to fall to the ground. Some even welcomed the blackness to descend. Eve's legs buckled, unable to stand the strain any longer.

The guards pushed their way towards her and began whipping. She felt nothing, she was laying on soft and warm cotton wool. She wondered if she had died and gone to heaven but there was nothing but fluff all around her.

Finally role call finished and Veronique and Marie went to her to carry her back to the hut. Veronique was pleased to see Marie taking an interest. The first sign she had seen since the beating that had broken the nun so completely. Carefully they carried the unconscious Eve to the hut and laid her on her bunk. Veronique checked she was still alive and breathed a sigh of relief. There was still life there but only with a faint pulse.

"She really needs a doctor," said Veronique.

Marie gave a harsh laugh and said, "You won't get that here."

"I know that," said Veronique. Her voice was flat, showing no emotion. She couldn't bear to lose Eve as well as Paulette especially so close together like that.

"This place is a killer," said Monique joining them. "Is she all right."

"What do you think?" asked Veronique, a harsh tone to her voice.

Marie looked at her quickly, wondering why Veronique should speak like that. Monique hadn't done anything wrong. Marie kept quiet, decided not to say anything. After all it could just be because of the close friendship Veronique had with Eve.

There was a faint groan from the bunk.

"Hello," said Veronique. "Can you hear me?"

Another moan. An arm twitched slightly but no answer. The three women looked at each other. Was there hope that Eve was coming back to them. They knew it was touch and go with her. Eve remained in her unconscious state but Veronique feeling for a pulse again felt it stronger.

"I think she'll be ok."

Marie and Monique breathed a sigh of relief.

"Why don't you two go and lay down. You need your rest for however long they'll allow us," said Veronique.

"What about you?" queried Monique.

"I'll stay here and watch her. I'll wake you if she takes a turn for the worse."

Monique hesitated but Marie pulled her away leaving Veronique alone with her friend.

Veronique began talking to her in a low tone so as not to disturb anyone. She implored her friend to fight and come back to them. She couldn't lose her as well. Who knew what would happen if she was still out of it by the time role call came. Would the Germans just shoot her?

Veronique must have dozed off because the next thing she knew was the sound for role call. She groaned and looked across at Eve whose eyes were open and staring up at the ceiling. There was no blinking which terrified Veronique. She felt for a pulse and there it was a stronger beat than before.

"How are you?" asked Veronique.

"Feel as if I've been run over," came the reply rather weakly.

"I'm not surprised. We were worried about you for a while."

"I hurt all over," said Eve.

"Hardly surprising with what we went through yesterday and then you were whipped for collapsing at role call. Talking of which we better get a move on before they come looking for us and you'll get it again."

Veronique helped her friend stand and walk outside. They slipped into place just in time. Veronique kept giving a sideways glance to Eve to make sure she was ok. It was obvious she wasn't but she couldn't be allowed to fall again. She wouldn't survive another beating so soon.

Marie watched and gave a surreptitious nod in Veronique' direction which was returned. Seeing Eve like that seemed to have stirred something in Marie again. She was reminded of all that had been done to keep Eve and the others safe and once again felt a sense of responsibility for her group of nuns. Even though Eve wasn't officially one of them she still felt it for her as well. Marie was coming back to them.

Monique noticed it. She wasn't sure how she felt about that as she had been hoping to be Reverend Mother when they were finally released, whenever that happened. She had never expected to find herself imprisoned by the Germans. She thought she would have some immunity. It wasn't to be and she felt betrayed, although she could still feel no hatred towards her captors who didn't know who she was and if they did couldn't award her any special favours anyway.

Chapter Twenty Six

There was a low hum of aircraft. The women didn't even look up. This was becoming a regular occurrence now. They were heartened by it and no longer took any notice of the German propaganda which they now recognised it for what it was. Lies!

They had become hopeful that release would come soon and free them from the German tyranny.

They had no idea how close the allies were to finding them and setting them free, but the Germans did and were becoming very nervous. They were waiting for orders which they were sure would come any day. Were they to shoot all the prisoners or were they to withdraw with them further behind the German lines?

At that very time the allies were making their slow way through France, liberating it a bit at a time. They knew the Russians were advancing closer to Germany on the other side.

One morning the women woke up to brilliant sunshine but no role call. They thought this a bit odd but after a brief discussion decided to stay where they were and wait for the inevitable sound. It didn't come.

Veronique, the bravest of them, decided to look outside. She took a few steps out and looked around amazement spreading across her face. She rushed back in excitedly.

"There are no guards anywhere. The Germans have gone."

All agog to know what was happening they rushed out of the hut and in a crowd started talking at once wondering what was happening, and not knowing what to do.

Hearing them, the other women left their huts and joined in the happy throng.

"Do you think they have left any food?" asked Eve quietly of Veronique.

"I don't know. I wouldn't be surprised if they've left us to starve to death. That would be the sort of thing they'd do."

Eve went back in to lie down, feeling too weak still to stay with the others. Marie went and sat with her not wanting her to be alone in case she should need something.

"Thank you for all you did to try and keep us safe," said Eve.

"You don't have to thank me. We were just doing what we could to help God's chosen people."

"You went far beyond that though. When you saw the situation you allowed me to join your number instead of staying hidden."

"I feel I failed you. Your daughter was captured and you have spent a couple of years in a camp."

"Maybe, but you still kept me safe. You could so easily have told the Germans I was a Jew which might have kept you much safer."

It was at that moment that Veronique walked in. She smiled at the two women.

"Marie, I hope it's ok to call you that, but Eve told me along time ago about the trouble you had at the convent. Have you ever realised who the traitor actually was?"

Marie looked up startled, "No. I assumed that we'd got it wrong and it wasn't any of us and must have been Julieanne after all."

Veronique shook her head. "Your traitor is here amongst you. I have been able to work it out from the little information Eve gave me. I didn't want to say before because it seemed irrelevant."

"How have you worked it out?"

"It was easy. One of your number has been a bit stand offish. Well, more so than the rest of you. Also I couldn't help but notice her joy when you started to withdraw. She thought she was going to get the chance to take over. If I'm right she could also be a member of the Nazi Party. She is the one person who is not celebrating along with the rest of us."

Marie stood up and went outside to see if she could work out who it could be. She paled as she watched, exactly as described by Veronique, one nun stood apart from the women with an unreadable expression on her face.

Going back into the hut Marie sat down quick. "I can't believe it," she said. "How could she do that to me. I trusted her."

"It's a mistake to trust anyone in these dangerous times," said Veronique.

"You don't understand. It's my fault. Everything that happened to bring us to the attention of the Germans was down to me. I told her everything, believing she was trustworthy. I would never in a million years have thought this of her.”

“Who is it?” asked Eve. She was feeling left out, not having a clue who they were talking about. She was surprised that Veronique had known for sometime who it was.

Marie shook her head, even now, unwilling to betray the traitor. Veronique having no such loyalty saw no reason to keep it to herself any longer and spoke the name, Monique.

Eve gasped. “Surely not, she’s been so kind to me.”

“It was all false,” said Monique walking into the hut at that moment and hearing the last part of the conversation.

The others stared at her. She seemed to have completely changed even her accent was different. It had always been very French but now there was a guttural sound to it, even though she spoke in the language and not in German, which was her native tongue.

“How could you?” asked Marie.

“Easily,” said Monique. “You mean nothing to me. I’m a good actress, always have been. It was decided I was the best person for the job as a spy for my country. My father is a high up official within the Party so I was known.”

“But you always seemed so helpful and caring,” commented Eve.

“Why would I help you? You’re just a filthy Jew. You should go back to the sewers where you came from,” sneered Monique, her voice filled with hate.

"You have no right to speak like that. Have you learned nothing from your time as a nun?" asked Marie quietly.

"A nun. Hah. I have nothing but contempt for you all," she said pulling her habit off. At least I know longer have to pretend to be someone I'm not."

"If you're really German, as you claim to be why were you sent here along with the rest of us instead of being set apart?"

"It was decided I would be caught out if I didn't stay imprisoned with you. We didn't want the resistance to work out who I was because then I'd be a marked woman."

Marie nodded, unable to find the words to say, and not sure she even wanted to speak to this woman who had caused so much damage and led to the deaths of several people, including Julieanne who had been killed as a traitor, erroneously it seemed.

They stopped talking, hearing the sound of vehicles in the distance. This was the first time of hearing anything outside the camp as they were miles from anywhere.

They rushed out leaving Monique behind.

No one spoke, listening as the sound got closer. They finally saw the army trucks approaching. It wasn't the German army either but the British army. The women as one moved to the gate and cheered. It was finally over. They were free.

Marie could start to take control back of her nuns. Monique, well she would be taken care of and dealt with by the British. Eve would begin the long search for her family to see if they had survived. She agreed to go back to the convent to recuperate and let them help.

Veronique knew she would always be friends with Eve. They would keep in close contact. She had been invited to the convent as well but she declined feeling uncomfortable in a religious setting. Her views of religion were enhanced by Monique's betrayal.

Marie was determined to reach out to all those who had been scarred by the Germans, not just the Jews. She wanted the convent to become a true haven of peace and healing, a place of safety.

www.ingramcontent.com/pod-product-compliance
Lightning Source LLC
Chambersburg PA
CBHW080358030726
47598CB00010B/2795